THIS IS NOT YOUR CITY

| Caitlin Horrocks |

THIS IS

N O T

Y O U R

C I T Y

| STORIES |

Sarabande  Books

LOUISVILLE, KENTUCKY

Managing Editor
Sarabande Books, Inc.
2234 Dundee Road, Suite 200
Louisville, KY 40205

Library of Congress Cataloging-in-Publication Data

Horrocks, Caitlin, 1980–
 This is not your city : stories / Caitlin Horrocks. — 1st ed.
   p. cm.
 ISBN 978-1-932511-91-8 (pbk. : alk. paper)
 I. Title.
 PS3608.O7687T48 2011
 813'.6—dc22

                    2010050304

Cover and text design by Kirkby Gann Tittle.
Manufactured in Canada.
This book is printed on acid-free paper.

Sarabande Books is a nonprofit literary organization.

This project is supported in part by an award from the National Endowment for the Arts.

The Kentucky Arts Council, the state arts agency, supports Sarabande Books with state tax dollars and federal funding from the National Endowment for the Arts.

For my mother, my father, my sister
and for Todd

CONTENTS

This Is Not Your City

Zolaria

It is July and we are a miraculous age. We have been sprung from our backyards, from the neighborhood park, from the invisible borders that rationed all our other summers. We are old enough to have earned a larger country, and young enough to make it larger still. The woods between Miller and Arborview become haunted. Basilisks patrol the Dairy Queen. We are so beset by dangers we make ourselves rulers over them, and by July we are the princesses of an undiscovered kingdom. We make maps with colored pencils. Here be Dragons, I write across the square of Wellington Park, at the end of our street. Here be Brothers, Hanna writes across her own backyard, and we avoid them both. We are too old for these games, too big for this much imagination, but we are so unpopular that summer that there is no one to care. We have finished the fifth grade alive and we consider that an accomplishment. We have earned this summer.

The neighborhood has been emptying of children. There are bigger houses being built past Wagner, past the edge of the western edge of town. The houses here, one story, one bathroom, have become a place to live after children or a place to move away from when they come. This year Hanna-Khoury-eight-houses-down and I are best friends, a thing I haven't had before and won't have again until I'm married, both of us twenty-four, an age my family will say is too young and I will be proud years later of proving them wrong.

3

That summer we pick blackberries in the Miller woods and take them to Hanna's house where her mother rinses them in a plastic colander. Hanna's parents still live together and their house feels friendlier than mine. When Mr. Khoury visited our fifth-grade class our teacher introduced him as a man there to talk about his "troubled homeland." He was a man from somewhere else, a troubled country people left and then called home, a country defined only by its perpetual unhappiness. Mr. Khoury told us that we were lucky, lucky boys and lucky girls, lucky American children, and Hanna rolled her eyes, embarrassed. Mr. Khoury has a Lebanese flag on the wall of his study and I think it must be a kinder sort of country that puts a tree on its flag. This is one of many things I do not understand that summer.

The gas station at the corner of Miller and Maple closes and there is a sign in the windows announcing upcoming construction, Project Managers Ogan/Veen. We don't know that the construction will never happen, that nothing will ever be built there, because the gasoline has leached into the earth 100, 200, 300 feet down, some impossible depth that no one will own up to and that can't be cleaned. That summer we ride our bikes around and around the empty gas station and look in all the windows. Hanna says Ogan/Veen looks like the name of a monster, and from then on he haunts our summer in a friendly sort of way, a goblin who lives in an empty Shell station and wanders the neighborhood at sundown. If we are lucky, he will encounter only the children who have spent the past year tormenting us, and he will grind their bones for bread.

"Ogan Veen, Ogan Veen,
His farts all smell like gasoline,
His stomach's full of children's spleens,
Ogan Veen, Ogan Veen," we sing. There are other verses but this one's my favorite because I've come up with "spleen" all by myself. Hanna doesn't know what it means and I'm not so clear either, but it rhymes and my mother's said it's a part of someone that can be eaten.

"If you're a cannibal, I guess," she said, and I said *perfect*.

On one of my dad's weekends, I ask him to take us to Dolph

Park, too far to bike to. The hiking path circles two lakes, Little Sister Lake and Big Sister Lake, and since I am an only child and Hanna has two brothers, we decide to split the lakes between us. We fight over who gets which. We are the same age and nearly the same size, although Hanna's arms and legs are gangly and seem destined for great height. In seventh grade, the year Hanna will slip a note between the vents of my locker that reads "I Hate You" over and over, filling an entire notebook page, I will be 5'2" and as tall as I will ever grow. My father is 6'1" and will call me "Midget." When I briefly register with an online dating site after college I will call myself "petite." Hanna will never grow tall, either, and because we can't know these things, we ask my father to flip a coin over Big Sister Lake. I can see him peek and scuttle the coin when I call heads, a move too quick for Hanna to notice. She cedes the lake to me, accepts the smaller for her kingdom, and I try to tell my father that night over carryout Chinese what I am only beginning to understand myself, that the way in which he loves me is not quite the way I wish he would.

In fifth grade Hanna and I doomed ourselves. On the second day of school we took out our folders, our pencil cases, organized our desks, and Hanna had space dolphins and I had pink unicorns. Two years ago all the girls had school supplies like this, and I don't understand why they have abandoned the things they loved. Hanna and I were startled but not stupid, and if no one had noticed us that day we would both have begged our mothers to take us to K-Mart that night and exchange them. But it was too late. We were the girls with the wrong school supplies, and everything we did after that, even the things that were just like everyone else, were the wrong things to do. I will never tell Hanna that space dolphins aren't really as bad as pink unicorns, and that she wasn't really doomed until I made her my friend.

The Little and Big Sister Lakes are the eastern edge of what we name Zolaria that summer, simply for the sound of it, the exotic "Z" and the trailing vowels like a movie star's name. The northwestern border is the Barton Dam. It takes us most of the summer to get there, sneaking closer and closer, up Newport

Road and through the grounds of what will be our junior high
school. One day there is a door propped open by the tennis
courts and we decide to explore. There is a sticker beside the
door: No Shirt, No Shoes, No Service. I am barefoot and we are
so timid this sticker foils our plan until Hanna takes off her left
shoe and gives it to me. Now we are within the law, and follow
a chlorine smell as far as the locker rooms, the labyrinth of
showers, the locked door to the pool. We hear footsteps and run,
directionless, past the library, the main office, the Cafetorium,
past the music room where I'll play flute for three shrill years.
Hanna will have quit band by then; Hanna has only so much
energy, her mother will tell mine on the phone, and doesn't want
to waste it on the trombone. We run past the glass trophy cases
in the foyer and finally we find the open door, the patch of blue
sky and red and green tennis courts. In the homestretch Hanna's
shoe flies off my foot and she yells, "Forget it! Don't stop!" but I
go back and we make it out anyway.

   The next day we bike through the junior high parking lot
and across the freeway overpass just north, where we yank our
arms up and down until three trucks have honked their horns.
We take our bikes into the nature preserve and ride them until
the hills get so steep they rattle our teeth. We ride bikes like
girls, throw like girls, we know it, and there is no one around
that summer to make us ashamed. We walk our bikes through
the forest, the sound of the freeway to our right and a creek to
our left, a symmetrical hum. Eventually there is a fence and a
gate and a dirt road that leads to the Barton Dam. We ride to
the huge gray wall of it, the rush of water at the base, the scum
scudding across the surface of the river like soap suds. There
is a dead animal floating at the base of the dam, bloated and
spongy and colorless. Its fur is breaking off in hanks, drifting
in the patches of foam. It is a cloudy day and we are alone on
the river path. A man comes out of the pump station at the top
of the dam and walks out along the wall. He leans against the
safety railing and shades his eyes with a hand and looks down
at us. We know we are in the borderlands, where our kingdom
meets a stranger's, where Ogan Veen wanders in daylight, and
where we should not linger.

∞

Thirteen years later, Cal and I will announce our engagement on Christmas morning over crumpled wrapping paper and freshly-squeezed orange juice. It will be the coldest morning of any year of my life so far, the paper's lead headline the temperature, 26 below, but as we unwrap presents we will see one of the Khoury boys outside walking their dog. My mother will call me into the kitchen to tell me I am young. "You're young," she'll say. "You're still so young."

"Not that young," I will tell her.

"Yes, that young. You barely know each other."

"I know him."

"You don't know yourself," she'll say. "That's what I worry about. How can you get married when you don't know yourself yet?"

"I know myself plenty," I'll say. "I think I know all I want to."

One night in July, Hanna and I have a sleepover and dream almost the same dream, in which Ogan Veen is chasing us, gnashing his long, stinking teeth. Zolaria is not his to haunt, so we build traps in the woods, stretch fishing line between trees, scatter tacks in the dirt and make piles of throwing-rocks in places with good cover. In my backyard is a half-dug decorative fishpond, a project my father started and abandoned, and we lattice the top with long sticks, camouflage it with leaves and cut grass. Every day I wait for Hanna to come up the street so we can check it together. I do not want to face our quarry alone. We bow branches, harp them with yarn, notch twigs and practice our archery. We strip the leaves from long tendrils of weeping willow and crack the whips in the air. We run shouting through the woods brandishing foam swords from a Nerf fencing set. We are girded for battle, but the enemy will not show himself. We catch nothing, but we have made ourselves afraid. It seems unfair, that a kingdom we invented should have its own mysteries, its unvanquishable foes. By September, we are almost eager for school to begin. We are tired of checking a dry fishpond for ogres every morning. But as princesses of Zolaria, we cannot say such a thing out loud. We have certain duties to our kingdom, to our adoring subjects. We must give the appearance of keeping them safe.

My father will take me once more to Dolph Park, when I am in high school, for old times' sake. The lakes are in the middle of an algae bloom, the weather hot and the water full of nitrogen and phosphorus. I will explain this to my father, nitrogen, phosphorus, when he grimaces at the damp mat of green over the pond, looking solid enough to walk on. My high school will have implemented an experimental science curriculum the year I enter tenth grade and I will know a great deal about eutrophication and very little about anything else. We will pretend to skip rocks but will really just be throwing things, stones and sticks and clods of dirt, watching them break apart the algae and sink out of sight. We will throw until our arms are tired and I will talk about the environmental benchmarks of healthy aquatic environments. We will get milkshakes at the Dairy Queen on Stadium Boulevard and two weeks later my father will move to San Diego.

In sixth grade Hanna and I will still be in the same Girl Scout troop. We will sing Christmas carols for the old people at Hillside Terrace nursing home, and in the spring we will sell cookies. I will sell enough to earn a stuffed giraffe, while Hanna sells only enough for a patch to be sewn on her vest. She will already be sick and I will have no idea. She will miss the whole last month of sixth grade, and four Girl Scout meetings, but it will be summer before my mother takes me to visit her. The hospital will remind me of a shopping mall, places to buy medicine and gifts and food, departments for having babies and looking after babies and looking after children and fixing all the different things that can go wrong with them. It is a weighty place but exciting, the way my mother asks the front desk for Pediatric Oncology and I press the button in the elevator.

Hanna's mother and mine will go for coffee, leaving us alone. Hanna will be wearing a violet-colored bandanna. She will say she is a gangster, and I say she would make the worst gangster in the world, which is true. She says a highwayman, then, which feels a little closer, and when I suggest pirate, we're off. We go once more to Zolaria, the bed rails marking the deck of our ship, and Hanna says climb on, that I won't hurt her, and our kingdom acquires an ocean, high seas. Aweigh anchor, we say, trim the sails, cast off, fore-and-aft, and we are all right for a time. We will be eleven, almost twelve; we will keep looking at the door, hoping no one comes in and sees us. After half an hour Hanna will throw up twice in a plastic tub beside the bed. She will say she leaned over to take a sounding, that the sea is a thousand fathoms deep where we are, that if we don't make it back to port we'll drown for sure. I will ask her if she wants some water. She won't say anything, but I'll fill a plastic cup from the jug on the nightstand.

"I had a dream the other night that Ogan Veen was back," I will say. "It was in the woods and he was chasing us and when we went out the fence we were saying, 'I don't hear him, I think we made it,' but then he was right there in front of us smiling and then I woke up." Hanna will look at me and her eyes will be dark and flat and I will know it was a terrible idea, to tell her this dream. She will sip her water and I will watch her sip it and we will wait for our mothers to come back and when they do we will be glad.

I will be unprepared for how long this sickness takes, for how long Hanna will be neither cured nor desperate. I will visit her once more at the hospital, twice more while she's at home. I will realize I am waiting for her to be either well or dead. She will feel very far away. I will start junior high alone, and when Hanna comes for her first day, in late November, I will be startled to see her. Our morning classes must all be different because I recognize her for the first time at lunch, sitting by herself. I will already be sitting in the middle of a long table by the time I see her, my lunch unpacked in front of me. I will be pressed tight on either side by people who, if asked, would probably say I am their friend. Hanna will be wearing an awful wig, stiff and styled like an old woman's perm. The hair will be dark brown, not black, and will no longer match her eyes. She will be pale and her face swollen and she will not seem like someone I can afford to know.

∞

The summer we are ten we sketch maps of our kingdom and outline its Constitution, its Declaration of Independence, its City Charter. In the end they all become zoological surveys. The Haisley woods harbor griffins, borometz, simurghs. There are dragons on Linwood Street, basilisks on Duncan who turn children to stone. We understand that we have no sway over basilisks and dragons; we understand that they are the minions of Ogan Veen. He has servants now, he has armies, and despite all our efforts Zolaria is not as safe as it was.

We make other lists, too, of "People Who, In Zolaria, Would Be Imprisoned In The Dungeon FOREVER." Hanna keeps adding her brothers' names to the list and then erasing them until the paper is ready to tear and I tell her to leave them off, if she's going to feel so guilty about it. We make a list of "Animals That Can Be Ridden: Pegasus, Centaur, Griffins, and Space Dolphins." We decide this is too charitable, and amend it to "Animals That Can Be Ridden By Us." We decide to hire young men to look after our stable of space dolphins, and when we deem ourselves a little older, and ready for love, we will notice the groomsmen and swoon. We prepare speeches of protest, in which we declare our unwillingness to marry foreign princes, our determination to follow our hearts, until we are disappointed to remember that in our kingdom we have no parents, and may marry whomever we choose.

Fourteen years later, when I marry Cal at a Unitarian church that four months later will be sold and remodeled into a bed and breakfast, Hanna Khoury's parents will still be living down the street. My father will fly in from San Diego for the wedding, and he and my mother will agree to pose for photographs together: them, them and me, them and me and Cal, them and me and Cal and Cal's parents, the symmetry of happy marriages. The Khourys won't be at the wedding because I won't have invited them. I won't have invited them because I'm scared of what Hanna might have told them. Not about the way I never sat with her at lunch or talked to her in band, or the way I didn't ever claim, precisely, not to know her, or the way I never said I did.

Not even the way her life got worse and worse and I did nothing to make it better. Or the way when I saw how bad things got for her in school I was glad we weren't still friends. The day I will worry she's told them about will be a Monday in February during sixth period, Phys Ed, one of our two classes together. Hanna will be excused from almost everything except changing. She won't have to run or throw or dribble or swim, but she will have to put on gym clothes. She'll try to get her sweater off and T-shirt on without disturbing her wig, but it will almost always catch, tip, slide to one side. Sometimes it will fall limp onto the bench between the lockers. One day Barbara Zabrodska will steal it and send it flying. Marti Orringer will catch it, and throw it to Naomi Sullivan, who will throw it to Elizabeth Dugan, who will throw it to Jamie Piakowski, who will throw it to Carla Deleon, who will throw it to Mary-Alice, who will throw it to Roberta, who will throw it to me. And instead of giving it back I will throw it to Andrea, who will throw it to Aisha, who will throw it to a girl whose name I don't remember, and another, and another, and another, because there will be thirty girls in sixth-period gym and I can't remember them all. Then Leah Campo will throw it to Kendra Danielson, who will throw it to Jasmine, who will throw it finally, accidentally, to Mrs. Pendall the gym teacher, who will have heard Hanna crying and come in the back way, through the showers. Mrs. Pendall will give Hanna back her wig and will send all twenty-nine of us to detention, where we fill the room and are sent out into the hall, along the wall like a tornado drill. The detention supervisor will make us crouch the rest of the period, tornado-style, on our knees with our foreheads almost touching the wall, our hands curled around the backs of our necks to protect our spines from flying shards of glass. My knees will hurt and I will think that if a tornado really did sever my spine and paralyze me for life, I wouldn't have to worry anymore about not doing the right things. I will think that the feel of her wig in my hand was like a gutted animal, empty and dry and bristling.

Hanna will be in remission by the next fall, but her parents will already have taken her out of Forsythe Junior High and placed her in a private school. I will not know when the cancer comes back. I will have discovered how easy it is to never see someone, even an eight-houses-down-someone, if you do not wish to see each other. When she passes away, my mother will find out from a newspaper obituary. She will come up to my bedroom, will still be deciding whether to tell me herself or just show me the paper. She will hand it to me and say, "There's bad news, honey."

It will be my first funeral, and my mother and I will go shopping for black clothing together. As we leave the mall I will thank her for paying, like she's bought me birthday gifts or new back-to-school clothes, and then to fill the silence I will say something about JV field hockey, and then my mother will drop the shopping bags in the middle of the parking lot and hold me tighter than she ever has or ever will again. At the funeral I will be so worried about avoiding Mr. and Mrs. Khoury and their sons that I won't have time to cry.

At the wedding Cal's mother will squint at me and ask if I'm really Unitarian, or just needed a cheap place for the wedding. I will tell her that I'm pagan, that I make burnt offerings to forest demons in the Bird Hills Nature Preserve. She won't laugh. Cal and I will go to Toronto for the honeymoon and three and a half years later the doctor will tell us to get ready for twins, girls. I will be terrified. It seems like a sign. It seems like a coin has already been flipped, and we will spend years waiting for it to fall. I will stare at my daughters in matching pajamas and wonder which one Ogan Veen will ask for. Which one he'll try to take. If he will give them ten years, if he will come calling sooner.

One winter the twins, bored, will unearth old photos in the basement: their baby pictures, our wedding, school portraits of Cal and snapshots of my elementary school birthday parties. The year I turned ten there was no one I wanted to invite except Hanna, no one I thought would come if I asked. In the picture there is a cake with ten candles and only two girls grinning above it—they look as if they should be lonely but are somehow perfectly happy. Madison will ask me who the dark-haired girl is, and I will get a look on my face that will make Sophie elbow her sister into silence. She is the perceptive one, I will think, the one who reads people. And then I will think, please no, not her. And then I will think, please no, I didn't mean the other one.

On a July morning the summer before the girls begin kindergarten I will ask them to get dressed in their swimsuits, pull old shorts and T-shirts on over. I will pack a bag with beach towels and dry clothes, and they will ask which city pool we're going to. Wait and see, I will say, and we will all climb into the car. I will drive down the township road that skirts the edge of Bird Hills Nature Preserve; it will be lined with condos but still unpaved. I will park at the lot downriver from the Barton Dam, and we will climb the wooden steps up to the calm pond above the pump station. We will leave the trail to slide down the embankment toward the water. The shore is reedy, the ground spongy with black, rank mud. We will stand ankle deep in the water, and Sophie will yelp when her feet start to sink. I will suggest a short swim, and the girls will look at me with horror. The water will smell warm and spongy and tattered curtains of algae will stroke our toes. Madison will hold her nose, and in the end, I have to push them in. It will be only a moment, I promise, a slice of a second, that I hold them under. And then I will be tugging at their hair and the backs of their T-shirts and wrestling us all into a heap on the grass above the reeds, and a woman on a bicycle will be standing on the embankment trail shouting at me that the pond is no place for swimming. The water isn't clean, she yells. She talks about nitrogen, phosphorus. I'm sorry, I will say. I didn't realize. It's such a hot day, the girls were so hot. They asked to go wading and slipped. My daughters will not contradict me, and the bicycle woman will leave, and I will bundle them into towels, warm and dry. At home we will all stand under the shower, all of us crowded together, and then eat ice cream in the backyard. I will ask Madison if she heard anything underwater, a gnashing of teeth, a creature with eyes like an oil slick and incisors like bread knives, long and serrated. I will tell Sophie that Ogan Veen has a laugh like I-94 and a stink like algae. I will tell her that I have introduced them now, the three of them, Madison and Sophie and Mr. Veen, and if they ever meet him they must run away. They must tell him that they are princesses, that they are mine, that I will protect them in the only ways I know how.

Cal will get home from work and while I cook dinner the girls will tell him what I did and Cal will shout and I will try to explain myself and Cal will misunderstand and talk to his parents about having the girls baptized at First Methodist. I won't know how to tell him that that won't help, that it isn't what I meant. I won't know how to tell him that I am still bracing for a day when Sophie complains of a headache that turns out to be something more, when Madison reels dizzily in gym class and the teacher sends her home with a concerned note. When a doctor has something to tell me he asks me to sit down to hear. I will be trying not to think about the possibility of a day when I will drive to the dam again, climb the stairs to Barton Pond and wade in. I will walk until I can hear the pressing silence of the water, the rushing, vacuous weight of it. I will say, "Mr. Veen, do you remember me?" I will say, "Mr. Veen, I once ruled a kingdom and left traps for you in the woods. Don't you want your revenge?" I will say, "Mr. Veen, you are an ogre and a thief and the patron saint of Julys, of summer Sundays, of miracles." I will say, "Mr. Veen, do not take my children."

And if he asks, and if I think it will help, and if I think it is truly what I have to do, we will be swimming and it will be July and we are a miraculous age. We are in Zolaria, we are children, our bodies are honest children's bodies. We are narrow and quick and we still fit in all our hiding places, the sun-wet hollows and the flowers in pink and purple and turquoise, all the damp colors of girlhood. We are riding our space dolphins, and either we can breathe the water of Zolaria or we are no longer breathing and it is July and we are a miraculous age and we are ten.

It Looks Like This

Mrs. Holtz:

I know this was a favor, like extra-extra credit, but if you give anyone else this assignment, maybe you could just let them retake the Hamlet midterm? You said you wanted to make this easy for me, that all I had to do was write a long paper about my life, about my mom and my sister and my friends, about where I live and what I do, and you'd give me credit for completing your English class. I really appreciate it, but I thought I should tell you that this wasn't all that easy. Not knowing what to say about Hamlet is one thing, but this was embarrassing, you telling me to just write what I know and me still not knowing how to go about it. I tried to use topic sentences. You said you'd show the paper around if I did a good job, try to talk my other teachers into giving me credit for their classes the semester I left, so I tried to put some math and science and stuff in for them. Fifteen to twenty pages is a lot, so I used some pictures. I hope that's okay. This was really hard for me, for a lot of reasons.

I. This is where I live:

 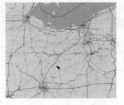 

←Waterton, Ohio

In the paper the other day, some guy said, "Based primarily on the strength of local tourism, Ohio's rural communities are sinking or swimming." My mom's the one who read it out to me, and she said, "Sinking or swimming? This fucking town was built underwater." I hope it's okay to put that. My mom's pretty foul-mouthed. She's been swearing more the sicker she gets. Now that she can't really manage the stairs, she's pretty obscene. What's happening to her is obscene, she says.

Maybe you could show this first part to Mrs. Steiner and Mr. Kincaid? My last semester I was taking Geography and Civics. They might like to see that I use maps and that sometimes I follow what's in the paper. I'm writing this at the library in Mount Vernon, and when the librarian asked what I was doing, I said I was writing a report, but with pictures. She said I had to cite some of them, like this: <www.openstreetmap.org>. That's where I got the maps from.

II. This is my house:

It's on County Road 54, and it stands out more than you'd think it would because the neighbors are all Amish. The ones to the east of us have always been there, but the ones to the west just moved in from Pennsylvania because the land's cheaper here. They cut off the electricity and dumped the kitchen appliances out in the yard. I'm tempted to ask if I can take the oven, because it looks newer than ours, but they're all so unfriendly. Besides, I'm not sure how I'd haul it inside.

It's an old farmhouse, but we never did much with it apart from a kitchen garden, a few chickens. The roosters are sons-of-bitches, and that's not what my mom says, that's what I say, because I'm the one has to go into the yard to feed them and they're trying to peck me to death. I have marks all up and down my legs. I'm looking forward to picking one out and eating it.

We knew it was coming, with my mom, and I said she should pick upstairs or downstairs, so we'd be ready when she couldn't go between anymore. I said if she picked downstairs we'd make do with the half-bath, but I was happy she picked Up. I have to help her wash now either way, but for a few months I could just get her settled in the tub and she could take care of herself. Now it's harder.

Since I mentioned them, here is a chicken:

And here is a plant from the garden:

I told my mom about your extra-credit idea, and she said to bring you tomatoes and zucchini from the garden when I bring this paper to you. I'll bring the tomatoes if they're ripe, but I'm embarrassed to bring the zucchini. Everybody's got it coming out their ears this time of year and giving it to someone just makes it look like you're trying to get rid of it. But I thought I should tell you that my mom said to bring you some, and that she said you're being very generous and that I should make sure you know that I appreciate it.

III. My best friends are Dana Linfield and Jess Berman. We sat in the back left corner, by the windows, in your American Lit class last year. They come by sometimes, but we don't have the same things to talk about anymore, so we just talk about old stuff, which gets boring. Plus it's hard for me to enjoy it when other people are at the house because I know that my mom's always waiting for them to leave. Dana's going to the Nazarene college in Vernon, and Jess answers the phone at a real estate office in Zanesville. Here they are:

You wouldn't know Elsa, and I don't have a picture of her. I think we might be friends, but it's hard to tell. I don't think she'd say no to a picture if I asked, because she's not really backward, like she'd think a camera was going to steal her soul. I just don't know how I'd ask her. Since I don't have a picture of her, here is one of her quilts:

I met her at the fabric store in Danville. Her husband brought her in their buggy. Elsa and I were inside looking out to the street when he tied their horse to a fire hydrant. I could hear her sigh and it made me like her. She's only a little older than I am, I think, but she has two kids. She does beautiful work. The fabric store always had some traditional pieces on display, but I hadn't realized they were hers until that day. She walked up to the counter and started unwrapping a puffy package, cut-up brown paper grocery bags tied with twine. It was just a Churn Dash, queen-sized, but done tiny, all by hand, the littlest pieces an inch square. "God," I said. "You'll go blind," which on one hand was an all-wrong thing to say to an Amish person, but on the other hand, you learn growing up around here that the Amish don't talk to anybody else anyway, so in a way it doesn't matter what you say to them. Elsa spoke to me, though. "Haven't yet," she said. "Don't intend to."

"I've had people asking after you," Mrs. Carpenter said. She runs the fabric store, and for a moment I thought she was talking to me, but it was to Elsa. "Up from Columbus for the day, antiquing. One of them owns a gallery on the Short North."

Elsa didn't say anything, just looked at Mrs. Carpenter. The look reminded me of how as a kid all the Amish on market days made me sad, because you could see how easily they smiled at each other but never at you, and I didn't understand what would be so wrong with me that I couldn't be smiled at.

"They asked who had done the Ohio Star in the window, and the Bear's Paw and the Trip-Around-the-World up on the wall. They asked me to take them down and match the stitching against the yardstick on the cutting table. Ten stitches per inch, they said, you don't see that much anymore. Is the whole thing by hand, they asked. And I said, absolutely, Elsa Beiler's Old Order, a real craftswoman. Lady said she'd be happy to carry pieces like these, and she knew someone with a traditional furniture shop in Olentangy who's looking for pieces to drape on bench backs, that kind of thing. She said you should bring some work by, since there was no way to call you."

"Wouldn't be much of any way for me to bring things by, either," Elsa said.

"Do you know anyone who could give you a ride?"

"I'd do it," I said. "I could take you."

They both looked at me. "Do I know you?" Elsa asked.

"No."

"Then I would pay you," she said, after a few moments thinking about it. "It would be a help."

"I'd be happy to," I said, and I was, maybe because she wore black sneakers with her navy blue dress, or because she spoke to me, or because it was a thing I could do that would get me out of the house, and after eighteen years growing up around people who wouldn't speak to me, I thought it would be nice to have one in my car for a while to talk to. We picked a day and a time, and she gave me directions to her farm, and when I got there it looked just like she'd said. It looked like this:

Every three weeks I drive to her farm to pick her up. I drive to the house, and she comes down the porch steps. She's always waiting on the porch. She's never had me inside and it keeps me uncertain if we're friends, or just friendly with each other. I turn the car around, then it's fifteen miles to the Interstate, forty minutes on 71 to this fancy Amish furniture shop in Olentangy, another half hour to the gallery in the city. People stare at her in Columbus, at her long dress and her hair pulled back hard under her bonnet, and I forget that I shouldn't be startled by it.

Elsa always has at least one new piece for each place, crib quilts and wall-hangings, small pieces to fill demand. Full-size bed quilts take too long. Still, she must spend hours every day away from the kitchen, or her children, or the garden, or whatever else she's responsible for, to produce that much work. I wonder what her husband thinks, what the other women think. In the car she talks about how in the autumn her hands are quick with a certain light, how they shake with the work inside them, and the only way she's found to calm them is to choose colors, cut pieces, load stitches on the needle. When she talks that way, it's the only time I feel sorry for her, but then I'm sorrier because it makes me happy to know that that's something I have that she doesn't, that if I ever wanted or found the time I could draw or dance or listen to music or just drive too fast with my window open and Elsa can't do any of those things. I didn't think she could have any music, either, until she told me she met her husband singing.

"It's just instruments we can't play," she said. "The teenagers have sings on Sunday evenings."

"Sing something for me," I told her.

"They're all hymns."

"Sing one anyway."

"I can't."

"Why not?"

"I'm married now. I can't sing anymore."

"That's sad," I said.

"Why? The sings are for courting."

"It's sad you had to stop."

"Why should I care what makes you sad?" she said.

The more I think about it, the more I think that Elsa won't let us be friends after all, and that's one more thing that makes me sad so then I stop thinking about it.

IV. I have a job. I make quilts too, like Elsa, but they're not as good:

If I sold this one as my work, handquilted at four to five irregular stitches per inch, some of the angles on the quilt top crooked and a few of the seams lumpy, it might bring $250

at Buried Treasures, in Martinsberg, $300 if it sold at Annie's Antiques, in Jelloway. $325 at the Treasure Mart in Danville. I'm not nearly as good as Elsa, and I'm definitely not Amish, which doesn't help in the quilt business. $250 minus $60 for fabrics, batting, and thread, divided by 150 hours of work, equals $1.27 per hour. This is why I don't sell my quilts as made by me.

To get technical for a minute, this quilt, with the crooked angles and the lazy handstitching, was machine-pieced out of salvaged, distressed, printed cottons, on an 1886 Singer treadle, filled with flat, all-cotton batting, and quilted with a size 7/9 needle using unwaxed thread. The pattern (Log Cabin: Barn Raising) was popular in northern Ohio from 1865 to 1895, and if I told you that's when this quilt was made, you'd have to know a fair bit about quilts to be able to prove me wrong. Antique quilts go for a lot—$500 minimum anywhere in Knox County, more in Columbus, but I'm scared to try and show in Columbus because the appraisers there know what they're doing.

I'm not sorry or anything. $500 minus $60 divided by 150 is still $2.93 an hour. I could do better driving to the Wal-Mart in Vernon, but I can't work outside the house because of my mom. She taught me to quilt years ago. I've always done it by myself. Quilting circles seem like a dumb idea. I don't want to sit around and listen to people bellyache. My problems are mine. No one else's. I've never really liked quilting all that much.

V. Please show Mr. Martin that I do math everyday now, more than I did when I was in his class. On my last sale, a double-size Dresden Fan, my hourly worked out to $3.438, but I remembered that when the last number is five or more, you're supposed to round up, and that makes it $3.44. I used a calculator, but please tell Mr. Martin anyway, and that I'm sorry I never understood logarithms. Also, maybe, that quilting takes a lot of geometry, and that I still remember that the Pythagorean Theorem goes like this:

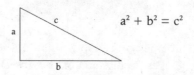

VI. This is my older sister, Melie:

    She's twenty-two, four years older than me. She's the pretty one, not that I think I'm ugly or anything, just that it's true, she's prettier. After she finished high school, she left Mom and me in the house to move in with her boyfriend in Vernon. She's still living there with a guy, but I lose track of who she's seeing. She still comes around sometimes and after she leaves Mom says, "If I'm not a grandmother yet, it's not for lack of Melie trying." I don't tell her that Melie could have made her a grandmother three times over, that I know of. Twice she asked me to take her to the clinic, all the way into Columbus, because she said people might recognize her in Vernon. I said if they did, they wouldn't find out anything they didn't already know about her. So the next time she had a friend take her, and I found out anyway, which goes to show that I was right all along. I don't know why the men don't take her. I don't know why she isn't more careful in the first place. I asked her once and she said what did I know, I'd never been with anybody and I acted like I never wanted to. "My heart's bigger than yours," she said. "You've got a skinny little heart inside."

VII. I don't have a picture of my mom. She wouldn't let me take one, but you can picture her kind of like Melie and me mixed up together except older, of course. She's got brown eyes and blond hair that used to be really long until she had me cut it a couple of months ago. I could tell she was sorry to cut it, but she was sorrier to need me to brush it for her, and tie it back, and this way probably works out better for the both of us.

Her hands got bad first, just hurting her and then hurting her so bad they got twisted up. Then her feet and her ankles did the same thing. The anti-inflammatories don't work the way they're supposed to for her. The doctors don't know why. She can't use her hands at all anymore, so I turn the TV on in the morning for her and turn it off at night. She can kind of use the remote control, but not so well, and she gets mad when she can't watch what she wants to. Her hands look like this:

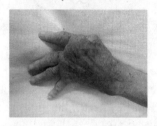

but those aren't her real hands. Here's the citation: <http://commons.wikimedia.org/wiki/File:Rheumatoid_Arthritis.JPG>.

VIII. Please tell Mr. Kincaid from Civics and US History that I remember that William Henry Harrison, who looked like this:

<http://commons.wikimedia.org/wiki/File:Harrisonwh-o.jpg>, served the shortest term of any president because he gave a long boring speech in the rain, caught pneumonia and died, and that the moral of the story is that we should keep it short. I remember that Gettysburg was the bloodiest battle of the Civil War but Antietam was the bloodiest day. I remember about how Manifest Destiny was both good and bad because the West was settled but lots of Indians died. I remember that Waterton was founded in 1841. I remember that in 1905, when the trains still ran, a boy died on the

trestle bridge near Gambier because his own father tied him down. I remember that our river is the longest in Knox County, that it is called the Kokosing and that this is an Indian word that means Owl Creek. Tell Mr. Kincaid that even when I'm on 71, heading home from the gallery in Columbus, and all I want to do is stay on the Interstate until it dumps me into Lake Erie, I think of it as our river.

IX. I thought about what I could put here for Mr. Samson, but I honestly don't do any physics. Not that I know of anyway, and I didn't understand it so well when we were learning it. I remember that gravity equals 9.8 meters over seconds squared, and that when something's falling as fast as it can possibly fall, that's called terminal velocity. Maybe you could tell him that I know about biology, even if I don't know physics. Like this: **K**ings **P**lay **C**ards **O**n **F**at **G**reen **S**tools: **K**ingdom **P**hylum **C**lass **O**rder **F**amily **G**enus **S**pecies.

X. Once in the car I told Elsa about my mom, about how she was sick. We talked about it a bit, and then Elsa asked me if my mom had a relationship with God. It was the only time Elsa has ever mentioned God to me. She said maybe it would ease her pain. I asked my mom about it that night, even though I knew it was a bad idea. "He's been fucking me over, if that counts," my mom said. "What's wrong with you?"

I want to tell Elsa what she said, but I'm worried I'll shock her, even though I've never seen Elsa shocked. I wonder if she'd have some suggestion, something I should say to my mom next, about God, or about Him having a plan, or about how things turn out okay in the end, or about not fighting so hard. I think of what Elsa could say to me, and I want to hear it from her, even if He doesn't, and things won't, and what else does my mom have left to do? Even if none of it's true, it would be nice to hear it from her, and believe it for a while, just as long as it takes to drive from Columbus back to her farm, and have it sound like a thing a friend would say to me, to have it sound like comfort.

XI. I think it was pretty soon after that that I saw you at the Kroger, in the aisle with all the cereals. You were buying Lucky

Charms, and it reminded me to ask about your kids. Then you asked about me, and you said it was a shame that I'd had to leave high school without finishing my last semester, when my mom got bad, and I said I guess, although I don't know what I'd do with a diploma anyway, since I'm not headed for college and I can't look for a job outside the house. And you said it would be a nice thing to have, it would just be an important, nice thing for me to have done. And then you told me to write this paper; you told me that you'd see what you could do.

I'm not telling you this because I think you've forgotten about it, but because it was a nice thing to have happen, it was just a kind idea for you to have had, and even if this paper doesn't turn out to be good enough, I wanted to say thank you.

XII. I've realized that I know lots more about biology. I know that my mom's hands are messed up because her synovium is swollen, which is the name for the lining around her joints. Her cells divide and divide and thicken the synovium and that's called pannus, and those cells release enzymes that eat bone and cartilage. I don't know if that has a name, but it means that her hands don't have the right shape anymore, because they're being digested from the inside, and even if the anti-inflammatories started working and she was in less pain, she'll never be able to use her fingers. I read somewhere, too, that pain travels through the body at exactly 350 feet per second, and for a long time I pictured the pain running from my mom's joints to her brain, over and over, racing with itself. Then I realized that the pain doesn't travel so much anymore as live there. It's settled on in, it's farming her bones, and it doesn't need to travel because it's never going anywhere.

I know that early-onset rheumatoid arthritis doesn't kill anybody, you just get older and your joints get more digested and there's nothing anybody can do for you. My mom's 45. She says, "I wish I had something that would kill me, sooner or later." I said, "Don't say that," and she said, "Wouldn't you, too? Or do you want to spend the next thirty years helping me off the toilet?" And of course I don't, but I can't ever, ever say that to her.

∞

XIII. The other day I showed up at Elsa's house to pick her up and she was waiting on the porch, like always, but her arms were empty. She waved me out of the car and up the steps and it was exciting, the feel of the wood stairs under my feet, even though they're just steps and just wood and I know they're not really any different from porch steps anywhere else. "I don't have anything finished this week," she said. "Nothing for the shops."

I almost said, "You could have called me," before I remembered that she couldn't. So I said, "That's okay," and asked if I should come back in another three weeks.

"I'm sorry you came all this way," she said, and I said I didn't mind. "Would you stay for some iced tea?" she asked. "Something to eat?" and I said I'd love to.

It was a nice day, sunny but not too hot, so it didn't feel strange that Elsa didn't invite me inside the house. I waited on the porch, and in a few minutes she came back out with two blue plates, glasses of iced tea balanced beside pieces of pie. The tea was kind of warm, no ice, and the pie was blueberry. We both sat on the porch railing, Elsa's skirt hitched up a bit, the forks clinking on the plates as we ate.

Please tell Mrs. Yarnell that I remember what she said in Life Skills/Home Economics about the Amish not keeping their kitchens clean the way a modern person would, and how we shouldn't buy their baking on market days if we valued our lives, but that I valued eating Elsa's pie on her porch along with my life and it's important to be polite. And also that the pie didn't make me sick or anything and that if Mrs. Yarnell could see the state of my kitchen at home she'd know it wasn't my place to be refusing anybody's pie.

I told Elsa the pie was good and she nodded at me. Every so often you could hear kids laughing inside the house, grasshoppers clicking in the yard. A fly kept trying to settle on the rim of my plate. Elsa stayed quiet until I was done eating and then she said, "You'll be all right."

"What?"

"You'll be all right. Even if it doesn't seem so, sometimes. You're going to be fine."

"Everybody says that."

"Like who?"

"Like my friends. My mom's doctors. My English teacher."

"That doesn't make it untrue."

"It's just a thing people say. They don't see how things will possibly turn out okay, but they want you to think they believe in you. That they believe that things will."

"It doesn't mean anything to me, whether you think I believe in you or not. Believe in you, what does that mean? You're not a ghost. You ate my pie."

"Sorry."

"For what? Eating my pie or being a fool? You're built for swimming," she said. "That's all I meant. You can believe as not whether God made you that way as long as you know you're not built to sink. You'll swim in this life if you want to, and if everyone keeps telling you so it's because they can see you've got fins. And a strong tail. And a mouth like this," she said, and pursed up her lips and went glub-glub like a fish, and I laughed. It was the first nice thing and the first joke she's told me, all at once, and the first pie and the first time talking on her porch, and I have hopes for seconds. Sometimes while I'm making dinner or piecing a quilt or writing this paper, I just sit and know that Elsa thinks I'm a fish, and that things turn out all right for all the swimming things in the world.

XIV. That just made me remember one more thing that Mr. Samson might like to read about. He taught us a lot about marine biology, so he might like to know that if I had the time to make any quilt I wanted, I would do a whole-cloth, the top all one color so if you saw it on a bed somewhere, you would think, how boring. But when you got up close, you'd see the trapunto stitching, the quilt top covered with animals in silver thread, one of everything that lives in the sea. Eels like snakes and the kind of jellyfish with tentacles that stretch for miles. Octopuses and giant squids, sharks and whales and coral and anemones and the kind of fish that live down where it's dark and have lanterns in front of their faces. I'd go to the library in Vernon and find pictures of everything, so I'd know what they all look like. I'd stitch made-up things, too, so there would be sea monsters and mermaids and sirens and kelpies. I'd like to put in Mimic Octopuses, too, but I'd have to figure out how because what's special about them is that they can look like anything. The quilt would be thick with everything I could picture, hundreds of secret creatures I'll never see for real. But only up close. From far away, it wouldn't look like anything, it'd just look like this:

Going to Estonia

Ursula Kotilainen left the north on January second, a Sunday. She'd already been on the bus for two hours when a boy with acne and a wispy mustache got on in Sodankylä and sat in front of her. He wiped the condensation off the window and waved frantically to an old woman outside, shouted as the bus pulled away. At a highway rest stop outside Kemi, the boy stood outside the men's toilets puffing out great gouts of air, trying to step forward into the clouds before they disappeared. He had a strange, flat face, and as Ursula watched him choke with laughter at his own breath she thought there was something wrong with him. But it was the first time she'd seen the sun rise in over a month, and as she looked at the boy, at the haze of exhaust the idling bus exhaled, at her own breath, she could believe that there was warmth in the belly of the world.

Back on the bus, the boy introduced himself. She told him her name and he wrote it unevenly in the moisture on the window, with the R pointed backward. "You're pretty, Ursula," he said.

She looked away; it wasn't true. He drew a heart around her name, and pressed his damp fingertip to the zipper at the collar of his coat. "Do you love me?" he asked.

"I don't know you," Ursula said.

"Tell me you love me."

"No."

"I love you." He was the first boy who had ever said this to Ursula, and the fact made her ashamed. He spoke like his tongue was swollen, as if he'd never learned to work it properly.

"No, you don't."

"Tell me you love me back." The boy unzipped his coat down to his belt. His face was flushed above the navy wool of his scarf and Ursula wondered for a moment if he might start crying, if he would howl the fourteen hours to Helsinki.

"I need to make up my mind. I'll tell you later," she said, and pulled a textbook from her carry-on. The boy set himself to wiping the mist off the windows with his mittens. Mittens, not gloves, Ursula noticed, even though he had to be sixteen at least, and perhaps as old as she was, a few months past nineteen. Through the damp, streaked spaces he hollowed, Ursula could see nothing but pine forest, dark and relentless. She was already as far from home as she'd ever been.

By Helsinki it was morning again, the sun rising earlier than it had in Kemi, the streetlights flickering off as the bus reached downtown during rush hour. "Have you decided yet?" asked the boy.

"I'm sorry. It would be bad luck to lie." Here in the south Ursula planned to get a degree, to meet men to whom she was not related, and to find a boyfriend. This damaged boy was not a good omen. It made her angry with him.

"So do you or don't you?"

"I don't." Ursula pushed forward down the aisle of the bus and stumbled out squinting in the sun. The bus driver pulled her bags from the luggage compartment and set them on the sidewalk. A middle-aged man and a woman, the boy's parents, Ursula thought, hugged their son and took his suitcase. He looked over his mother's shoulder as she held him and glared at Ursula. "I still love *you*."

"Don't," she told him.

Ursula was entering the civil engineering program mid-year, too late to receive university housing; the department had found a studio she could afford in a neighborhood of gray apartment blocks. Her neighbors on either side were Somali, resettled refugees. Ursula was not used to seeing black people; she thought they looked dark and strange against the snow, like holes in the world. When Ursula got off the tram in the evenings she'd pass a crowd of Somali boys playing on the sidewalk. They'd learned a Lappish song in school the same day they asked where she was from, and when she told them, they sang it to her. *Poro-tyttö,* they sang, *Reindeer Girl,* and laughed. The older boys still had an accent, and the language opened up in their mouths, loose and uneven. Ursula had an accent too, a northern one, but she spoke too seldom for most people to notice.

Jukka lived on the floor below her and stood on his balcony in the evenings with a cigarette, smoke disappearing up into his laundry. He hung the clothes wet and they froze stiff and solid in the cold, flapping and clacking like heavy wind chimes. He always looked down and waved as Ursula walked up the front steps to punch in the door code. He had bright hair and a quick face that looked either happy or very tired. Ursula couldn't tell how old he was. Happy, he was handsome, shiny like the actors on Swedish soap operas. She liked to see him happy. Sometimes they would chat at the tram stop and he would make her laugh out loud.

As the weather eased in February, the snow still hard but the cold a little gentler, she began to walk home from campus. Several kilometers, but there was a path that skirted the edge of Töölö Bay. For a week now enormous forest fires had been burning in Russia and the air smelled of smoke. Something else Yeltsin couldn't manage, putting out his own fires, and now there would be ash falling on Savo if the winds didn't shift. Ursula liked smelling the air and watching the ducks that gathered under the footbridge at the edge of the pond. Beneath the bridge a culvert trickled water onto the ice, melting a dark pool where the ducks could swim. They stepped off the edges of the ice and pressed into each other, crowding, the warm water invisible beneath the carpet of ducks' backs. She watched them until her feet began to numb in their boots, and she turned to leave. Her neighbor Jukka was standing behind her.

"I thought I recognized you," he said. "Headed for home?"

"I stopped to watch the ducks."

"Wait until summer. There'll be birds worth looking at then. For two, three months, anyway."

"Two months longer than I'm used to."

"Where are you from?"

"Near Inari."

"That far north?"

At home, Ursula thought, the sun would have barely made it above the horizon. The ice on the lakes was still getting thicker, pressing the fish down to the bottom where the oxygen would start to run out in April, when the thaw was still two months off. Years when the ice came early or left late, she could picture the thin crust of fish, silver and gasping.

"Do you have people there?" Jukka asked.

"All my people are there."

Jukka turned out to be from Kajaani, ten hours north instead of twenty. Two hundred years ago they had exported barrels of tar, Jukka explained, and now they exported nothing. "I came south for work. I got sidetracked. By the not-working. I've had a lot of that." He paused and changed the subject. "There are a lot of refugees in this neighborhood. You should watch out."

"Are they dangerous?"

"No."

"Then why should I watch out?"

"I'm just trying to be friendly." He smiled and Ursula thought she must look silly walking beside him, soft and squat as she was, almost a foot shorter, with heavy eyebrows so dark they made it look as if she dyed her hair, even though her hair was never lighter than wet sand, even in the long light of summer. Her grandfather had kept reindeer, and when they visited him as children her brothers had said she was like the animals, short and sullen and shaped like a pickle jar. When he died, the herd was sold, and her grandmother moved into an apartment in Ivalo, where Ursula's aunts and uncles had found work at the ski resorts.

"You're a student?"

Ursula nodded.

"You should come out for a drink some evening. My favorite

bar's on your tram line, a couple stops short of the university. MustaLintu. Off Kaisaniemenkatu, right downtown."

"I'd like that. Is there a night, or a time. . . ?"

"Just stop by."

"But when?"

"Some evening. Any evening you want. I'm there on all of them. Afternoons, too." He laughed then, and started a string of jokes, about Somalis, about Russians, about Estonians, about how they couldn't make sandwiches or use toilet paper or go back to whatever countries they came from, and then Ursula couldn't be sure he hadn't been joking the entire time.

A couple of weeks later Ursula worked up the courage to try and find Jukka at the bar. She wanted to wear a skirt, planned ahead and bought woolly stockings to keep her warm enough, soft white ones to wear with her tallest boots and a brown skirt that fell to her knees. After her civil engineering lecture, a survey course in geo-technology, she went to the women's bathroom in the basement where no one would disturb her. Not that anyone ever disturbed her, in hallways or restrooms or anywhere else; the other students had been in classes together since August and had not seemed to notice the new girl who slipped in and out of seats at the back of classrooms, who took the tram away from campus in the evenings to another part of the city. In the bathroom Ursula fumbled with makeup she had bought at the same discount store as her stockings. She put on eyeliner, then tried to wipe it off. It smeared but wouldn't fade, and in the fluorescent light she looked like someone had hit her. She pulled a long curtain of brown paper towels from the dispenser and scrubbed hard. The eyeliner came off but left her eyes looking raw and mournful, as if, Ursula thought, no one had ever cared enough about her to get around to wanting to hit her, which was close enough to true.

MustaLintu was on a grotty side street that took Ursula several tries to find. When she pushed open the door, she could recognize Jukka from the back, from only the line of his shoulders and the fall of his white shirt, pale in the dim light of the bar. He was standing with two white-haired men, slotting coins into a lotto machine. The machine whirred and Jukka read out cherry-cherry-grapefruit. The older men swore, until one turned and saw her and elbowed Jukka. At the bar he bought a beer for her and Coke for himself. He showed her to a small table near the front window and held the Coke down by his knees while he unscrewed a flask and asked about her classes. She told him about radial cable-stayed bridges, about lenticular trusses and cantilever spans, about the Howe-trussed bridge that connected Tornio and Haparanta and how since it was built Finns and Swedes from the neighboring towns had begun to marry each other and raise children whose voices were muddy with two languages. She talked until she realized she'd gone on far too long. "I'm sorry," she said. "What about you? What do you do?"

"I'm between jobs at the moment. I hang out a lot with Pekka and Jaakko here," he said, twitching his hand out behind him, where Pekka and Jaakko were still spinning mismatched fruit.

"What did you used to do?"

"Not much of anything, really. I've gotten good at hanging around the Job Center applying for things." He said this brightly, as if it were one of his jokes, and Ursula wondered if the fact that he didn't seem to mind not working meant that she shouldn't mind either. "Let me get you another beer."

Ursula watched him at the bar, where the bartender snapped the cap off her Lapin Kulta but put up a fight over Jukka's Coke. The argument was too soft for Ursula to hear, but Jukka pivoted away from the bar so fast he tilted and put his hand on a stool to steady himself.

"Don't know why the bastard won't cut me some slack. One of his best customers."

"Why not just order a real drink?"

"I'm a little short at the moment."

"Let me," she said, and he shook his head and laughed; this time it was at her, not at the Somalis or the Russians, and she felt bad for not knowing the rules, for offering something so ridiculous.

They took the tram home together, and Jukka walked up the extra flight of stairs to see her to her apartment. She shuffled in her boots as long as she could, her head tilted upward, but he did not kiss her. Once the door was locked behind her, she thought of the things she wished she had known how to tell him. How she was not pretty but not unaccomplished. How her grandparents had known how to herd reindeer so they ran angled, uphill, not panicked and in a straight line for miles ahead. How to milk, and butcher, and skin. How now her parents only knew how to take tickets for the ski-lifts at Saariselkä; her aunts and uncles, how to rent snowboards in Ivalo. How she had known how to lead tourists on snowmobile safaris for reindeer, and how to fake surprise when the reindeer appeared, penned where the tourists would be sure to see them. How she had not yet learned how to dress like an elf and press the buttons that operated the indoor roller coaster at Santa's World, as her oldest brother did, or how to sit in a bar in Rovaniemi and drink unemployment like her other brother did. How it had seemed very important to her to learn something new, things no one in her family had done, living in a city, riding a tram to college classes, calculating the load-bearing properties of an orthotropic beam.

A week later Jukka knocked on her door and asked for 200 markka. "Groceries for the weekend," he said. "My government money comes Monday. I'll go to the bank and pay you back right away."

In their language without the word please, that was all Jukka said, but the impatience was there, and the pleading. Ursula had stayed late at the university and the state-run Alko would be closed in half an hour. The Number 12 tram came in five minutes and then not at all. "200 markka, *ole hyvä*," Jukka said. *Be good. Be kind.* Ursula gave it to him.

That night Jukka knocked on her door holding a bottle of Koskenkorva and two shot glasses, wearing a T-shirt and a towel wrapped around his waist, his hair damp from the sauna. Ursula had been a few times, to the large sauna in the basement of the building, and seen Jukka's name written sprawlingly on the sign-up sheet across huge blocks of time, weekday nights and weekend afternoons.

"You shouldn't drink in the sauna," she said.

"Bad for the heart, I know," Jukka said. "But vodka and sauna. What more could a body want?" He said it like a proverb, a slice of wisdom, and Ursula wondered if it was a saying she'd never heard. "A pretty girl, maybe."

"Maybe you should go home."

"I'm sorry. I didn't mean anything by it. I just wanted to offer you a drink."

"I don't drink Kossu straight."

"I brought you this," Jukka said, and from the fold of the towel at his waist pulled a plastic bottle, tiny, like from an airplane or hotel minibar. The cloudberry liqueur was the same yellowy-orange of the berries that grew in the far northern swamps. He poured it into one of the shot glasses and handed it to her. He poured himself a shot of Kossu and toasted her as she stood in her doorway, Jukka barefoot in the hall. The liqueur was thick and syrupy; Ursula could feel it coat her throat, the taste of sugar and plastic and the slight hint of cloudberries, the sweetness without the crunch of seeds.

Jukka smiled at her. "Did you like it?"

"Thank you," she said.

There were other gifts, slipped through the mail slot in her door. A chocolate bar; an article torn out of the *Helsingin Sanomat* about a new bridge being planned for the Millau Viaduct in France that would be the tallest bridge in the world; a fashion magazine addressed to Jukka's neighbor on the second floor. Ursula went downstairs and pushed it back into the woman's mail slot, where the thick magazine stuck partway out. An hour later Jukka brought it back to her.

"I wanted you to have it," he said.

"It's not yours to give."

"If you don't want it, you should just say," he said, sulking.

She looked forward to the gifts, jumbled with sales circulars and bills. Her letters from home were short and infrequent. In the north there was a general economy—of light, warmth, money, jobs, events of interest; only so much of any one thing. She tried not to be annoyed at her parents' economy of language, at the letters on single sheets of paper, one-sided, in large, bubble-shaped script, variations of fine and weather and hope you're well and see you in the summer.

One evening a folded piece of paper whispered through the mail slot and fell onto the floor. She'd been sitting on her bed working out equations, replicating the numbers that had built the cable-stayed bridge in Heinola. She had driven over the bridge on the bus to Helsinki, and remembering it, tall and gleaming for years already, made her homework feel pointless. The delivery was folded to open like a greeting card. On the front it said, *You Are Invited.* . . . Inside it said, . . . *To The Booze Cruise! Join Jukka Tullinen and friends for a duty-free cruise to Tallinn on Saturday night, March 1st. Your ticket will be paid for.* There were clip art pictures of a rowboat and a bottle with three Xs on the label. On the back was a handwritten note: *I'm doing my mandatory hours at the Job Center. They've got me training on computers, so I made this invitation. I know it's retarded. The trip's for real, though. Let me know if you want to come.*

Ursula changed out of her slippers and flannel pants into a skirt. She couldn't decide on shoes and so left her feet bare. She shivered in the hallway as she waited for Jukka to come to the door, her spine rigid and shoulders hunched. It was snowing again, the wet flakes sticking to the window in the stairway landing. They stained the asphalt more quickly than the metal of the tram tracks and the rails stayed dark and metallic, threading beneath her through the white streets.

"You're going to Estonia?" she asked Jukka when he answered his doorbell.

"Sort of."

"How do you sort of go to Estonia?"

"The ship stays in the Bay of Tallinn overnight, but you can't go ashore or anything."

"Then what's the point?"

"The point's that it's the booze cruise. The whole deal is that the ship stays out in international waters long enough to sell stuff tax-free. You can save hundreds of markka."

"So you're taking a whole cruise to buy cheap liquor?"

Jukka blushed. He seemed brushed by shame at the oddest moments. "There are other stores, too. You can buy candy and potato chips and shirts and things. There's a lot of perfume. If you wanted perfume. I'd really like for you to go." Ursula had never in her life been taken for a girl who might want to shop for perfume. It was flattering, she thought, but so unexpected she wondered what she looked like to Jukka, how impossibly addled his vision of her might be.

"Can I think about it?" Ursula asked.

"Of course," Jukka said, grinning. His teeth were straight and even but yellow. Ursula thought it seemed a fair balance. "You don't really want to go to Estonia anyway. It's all babushkas and prostitutes and unpasteurized beer. The women there, they have it in for Finns. Friend of mine left a club, woke up in a bathtub full of ice with a kidney missing and a note in lipstick on the mirror."

"That's an urban legend."

"I swear to God. Lipstick on the mirror."

"It never happened."

"Have it your way. But if it did, Estonia's just the place it would. You're better off onboard. Trust me."

In her apartment that night Ursula put her homework aside and wrote a letter to her parents. For the first time she mentioned her handsome neighbor, who slipped presents through her mail slot. *We've been out a few times,* she wrote, trying to sound nonchalant. *He's invited me for a cruise. We're going to Estonia.* Ursula thought of the boy from the bus ride south, his slow tongue and strange face and damaged brain, and wanted to laugh at him, to tell him that he had not been the unlucky charm she feared. She had no need now for his mindless love; already, she'd found something better.

It took two trams and a city bus to get to the harbor and the Silja Line terminal. As they waited in line to embark, Jukka told her he had good news and bad news: bad, that his friends had bailed and it would be only the two of them; good, that he had shelled out for a cabin. The communal sleeping room was good enough for him; he'd once traveled to Latvia sleeping in a stairwell. But Ursula, he said, deserved to have a cabin. On the ship he led her down long pink and turquoise halls, low-lit and empty. There was a mirror on the back wall of their room, and two long, green upholstered benches, with latches above that held the bunks folded to the wall. In the small bathroom Ursula took off her woolly stockings and replaced her boots with heels. Her legs were pale and wobbly in the new shoes. When she folded the bathroom door along its runners, Jukka's face stayed tired. "I thought we'd get our shopping done first," he said. "Then we can do what we want."

The shopping mezzanine had long, glass windows that looked out on the Baltic Sea. Where ships passed, the ice was broken into plates, floating in dark canals that stretched through the sea like the damp-barked trunks of pine trees, the long dark legs of moose. Beyond the shipping lanes the sea was frozen white and flat and solid like tundra in every direction, west to the spray of islands of the Stockholm archipelago; and to the east, where the sea became the Neva as it swept into St. Petersburg. Ursula wanted to tell Jukka about the river she'd only read about, bound by bridges that could break their own backs, split to allow ships to pass. They were raised every night in rotation, trapping people in different quadrants of the city for hours at a time. Cars would race through the icy streets to make the last few minutes of a crossing: a city ruled by bridges.

They went to the liquor store first, where you could buy not only bottles but cases, and little luggage carts with bungee cords to wheel the cases away. Jukka took a cart and opened the duty-free shopping pamphlet, the maximum tax-free allowances illustrated with what looked like a child's drawings of adult sins, chunky red sketches of the possible permutations: Spirits + Wine OR Champagne + Cigarettes! Jukka put the pamphlet in his pocket and began hefting case after case, bottle after bottle, into the cart, breaking all the rules. Ursula was going to say something when he asked to have her boarding pass.

"I think I left it in the cabin. What do you need it for?"

His nose wrinkled like she was a smell he couldn't place. "You need to show your boarding pass at the register."

"I wasn't going to buy anything," she said. Then she looked from the full cart to his face, which was almost angry, and thought of all the floors she'd known that could actually swallow people up. Lake Inari in September or June. The Karasjoki river in November or April. The northern marshes that would drink you feet first in any season. The sea surrounding them now, the shifting ice, the slits of black water. The floor of the cruise ship liquor store had not been one of them.

"You need the boarding pass to buy my tax-free allowance. Of course. You planned on buying up two people's allowances. Save hundreds of markka. I'm sorry. I'll run and get the pass."

"It's back in the cabin?"

"On the bench, I think."

"I'll get it. Watch the cart," he said, and he was gone.

Once the liquor was stowed in the cabin, roped onto two separate hand trolleys and wedged under the benches, Jukka took her by the hand and led her back to the shopping mezzanine, into the cosmetics store. "Pick something out," he said. "Anything you want."

"I don't wear makeup. Or perfume."

Jukka insisted and Ursula circled the glowing counters, calculating how much Jukka's guilt could cost him. At the back of the store there was a tiny basket filled with clearance tubes of lipstick, lichen reds and bruise purples. She picked the brightest and dropped it into Jukka's palm. It cost eight markka.

"You don't really want this," he said.

"Sure I do."

"I really am glad you came. I wanted you to come. I want you to have a good time. It wasn't just the duty-free stuff."

"Please, just buy it and we can go back to the cabin."

Jukka paid and explained that the restaurants on board were expensive, that they should load up on duty-free snack foods. In the cabin they sat on the floor and ate handfuls of potato chips and cheese curls, bars of chocolate clotted with nuts and dried fruit. Jukka took the clear plastic cups out of the bathroom and filled one with vodka and orange juice, the other with straight vodka. He raised his cup and toasted cheers. They ate and drank until they felt ill and then Jukka kissed her. He tasted like the rubbery buttons of *salmiakki*—black licorice crusted with salt. Ursula decided she didn't mind.

They were both drunk when Jukka decided he wanted to check out the dance clubs. They left the cabin and Ursula ran her fingers along the wall as they walked. She imagined she could feel the enormous ship rocking, the cradled heaving of the Bay of Tallinn. The clubs, one floor down from the shopping mezzanine, were all playing the same EuroPop. Jukka kept drinking from a flask in his pocket, and Ursula kept closing her eyes to steady herself. When the strobe lights flickered she held her stomach. Jukka grabbed her wrist and listed, let his weight drag them onto the dance floor. He rested his arms on her shoulders and pressed his forehead down onto hers. Ursula told herself to make it to the end of the song, then, when Jukka pulled her closer, to make it to the end of one more. The songs all sounded the same, bright and thumping, and she lost track of how long they'd been there before she told Jukka she needed some air.

"I'm sorry," she said, when Jukka frowned. "I'm not feeling very well." She towed him out of the club, tripping through the plush carpet of the hallway. The glass doors to the deck strained against the wind, and Jukka had to help her shoulder them open. There were couples leaning against the railing, huddling together against the cold. Ursula walked past them toward the bow of the boat, the empty viewing area full of white observation chairs and sea spray. It was a new moon, pale and thin as an eyelash. The harbor lights glared in the dark. Farther out in the bay were freighters and another cruise ship, painted red and white and strung with lights. On land there were stacks of shipping containers like a child's game, towers of red and brown blocks. She could see the wind catch the thin layer of snow on the pavement and blow it into ripples, like sand.

When Tallinn had been part of the Soviet Union and Ursula had been a child, she had watched news reports of the city, filled with exotic exiles from Soviet territories. She would go there someday, she had dreamed, and meet a Mongolian in a long, red, felt coat lined with yak fur. They would fall in love and they would both be so clever they could learn each other's languages, and they would be finally so in love that they would not need languages at all. He would have his cousins in Ulaan Bator send her a matching coat and soft cashmere sweaters. They would move to the Black Sea and live in a dacha on the shore year round, and their children would only know what winter was like if she found the words to explain it. She thought about telling Jukka all this, and then pushed the story back down her throat, held it in her lungs with the air so cold it burned.

The wind had picked up and caught the white plastic chairs, flinging them backward against the wall at the rear of the deck. Ursula and Jukka had to dodge them, the chairs turning end over end or sliding along upright, four legs to the ground, as if invisible people were still sitting in them. Jukka caught a chair mid-flight and sat down heavily, anchoring it in the middle of the deck. He pulled Ursula onto his lap and put his arms around her. "Let's go inside," he said, and Ursula, out of breath, the wind freezing her chest, nodded yes.

They made it back to the room with Jukka's arm tightly around her, their feet colliding, hips joined as in a three-legged race. Jukka released the latches that held the bunk against the wall. It crashed down on top of the green sofa-bench, and Ursula heard the bag of cheese curls crunch. The bunk was already made up, tidy with sheets and a pillow. Jukka pushed her backward onto the bed, and she felt silly when she bounced on the mattress like a child's ball. "I like you," he said. "Really."

"Don't say that."

"What? I like you."

"I don't think you do," Ursula said, but part of her thought that if she'd believed him this long, if she'd even pretended to, she should see the thing through. He wanted her enough to lie to her. Perhaps that was something.

While she puzzled at what she should do she did nothing, and then Jukka was between her legs, her skirt pushed up and her underwear gone, Jukka's pants down but not all the way off. She could feel the heavy denim bunched somewhere around his calves, crowding her ankles. She opened her legs wider, feeling for a moment that his jeans were the part of him she could not bear to touch.

"Goddammit," he said, pressing against her. Ursula turned her head to the side. Jukka was still soft, even as he pushed at her, even as he grabbed at himself, his face red and his eyes unfocused. Ursula did not move to help him. "Drank too much. Drank too goddamn much," he said, shoving against her helplessly. Finally he dropped his head against her chest and apologized. Ursula reached her hand up and touched his cheek. "It's okay," she said, and was relieved.

Jukka fell asleep and Ursula found her underwear, smoothed down her skirt. She got down on her knees to clean the food off the carpet, scraping broken cheese curls and splinters of chocolate into her palm. She found the tube of lipstick under a potato chip. Uncapping the tube, she stepped toward the mirrored back of the room until she was nose to nose with her reflection, chapped lips and pale skin and her funny dark eyebrows. She began writing with the lipstick on the upper-left corner, above her ear.

> *Jukka,*
> *Have taken your kidney and gone to Estonia. Seek*
> *medical attention ASAP!*
> *Ursula*

On the bed Jukka was asleep on his stomach, his breath a liquid snore. She pushed his shirt up and he didn't stir. She pressed one hand to the small of his back, wondering where his kidneys were, what they looked like. She drew an oval to the right of his spine and rubbed the blunted end of the lipstick with her index finger, drew the finger across her lips. She kissed Jukka's back in the center of the kidney. "I'm going to find the sleeping area. I'll get home just fine tomorrow. Don't worry about me," she whispered, her mouth moving against his skin. She was embarrassed after saying it that she had imagined Jukka worrying about her, that his sleep might be troubled by her absence. "Goodnight," she said, pulling a blanket from the other bunk to cover him.

Ursula found the sleeping room on an upper deck, a humid and windowless space lit by two red EXIT signs. Passengers cocooned in coats and jackets sprawled on benches and pressed into corners. Ursula waited for her eyes to adjust to the dimness, threaded her way through the sleeping bodies. She found a narrow patch of floor between two anonymous shapes, men or women, their faces turned away; she stretched herself out on her side with her backpack wedged under her cheek. The stranger behind her jerked and flung a hand out, its fingers brushing the nape of her neck. Ursula lay still. She thought of her pretend Mongolian husband and of their little house on the Black Sea, where the summers were long and warm and lit and their breath would be invisible. She slowed her breathing to the quiet pace of the bodies around her, the warm animals curled in the darkness. She imagined the feel of her own vertebrae under the stranger's fingers, and found herself hoping that the hand wouldn't move until morning.

Zero Conditional

Principal Steckelberg was late. Eril brushed snow off the wooden steps of the administrative portable and sat to wait for him. Morningcroft Montessori Academy was made up only of portables, standing in a circle on concrete blocks. In her phone interview, the principal had told her that the portables were the same colors as the pie wedges in Trivial Pursuit. This, he had said, symbolized the value Morningcroft put on knowledge. When he arrived he unlocked Cerulean, where Eril would be teaching the third grade.

"Fourth grade is in Vermilion, second Lemon, first Tangerine, fifth Salmon. We have an excellent teaching staff. They'll be a real resource for you." Steckelberg opened the door and stood aside, gesturing toward the darkened classroom as if presenting a prize she had won. Eril supposed she had. It was a job, after all. The heat had been off for two weeks and she could see her breath. A long table below the windows on the opposite wall was covered with cages of hamsters, a rat, a fish tank, a tiny garter snake under a heat lamp.

"Your predecessor was quite the biologist. We're sorry to lose her. She had a last-minute job offer after Christmas. Some kind of fieldwork out in New Mexico, dietary habits of predatory birds. She was coming in to feed the animals up until yesterday."

On the table, Eril's predecessor had left long lists of instructions on the care and feeding of the animals. She had also left bowls of soft gray balls of owl vomit filled with the fur and bones of whatever the owl had eaten. The contents of twenty pellets had been glued, spread-eagled, on squares of cardboard, the bones arranged into the skeletons of voles and shrews. It was an ambitious project for third graders. The skeletons were caked in Elmer's glue, slivers of rib bones shellacked onto skulls, paw bones the size of rice grains wedged into eye sockets. Larger bones were scattered across the table, sticks and bark and the jagged brown dust of dried leaves, sea shells that smelled like the residue of the animals they'd harbored, damp and rotting and salty. It was a great wreckage of life.

Steckelberg left and Eril walked across the room to the table. The portable felt suspended over some uncertain, hollow space. Once she heard the principal's car pull away, wheels spinning in the unplowed lot, she jumped up and down. The floor quivered. Eril was not used to feeling so large. She looked at the walls, the alphabet in cursive, the American flag, a series of Your State Symbol posters: the official fish of the state of Michigan was apparently the Brook Trout, the official mineral the Petoskey stone. The official state game animal was the White-Tailed Deer, for which, she read, the hunting season was divided into periods for Archery, Regular and Late Firearm, and Muzzle-loading. She wondered if her eight-year-olds would know these things. She wondered what she was supposed to teach them. For a moment she wanted to cry.

Monday morning she stood and watched the children arrive, stripping off their coats and boots in a pile near the door. The children stared at her suspiciously and read her name, *Ms. Larcom,* on the blackboard along with the date and a Word of the Day: *fortitude.* A boy lifted the rat out of its cage and cradled it in his hands, letting the long, hairless tail dangle in the air like a tentacle. "Binx's tumors have gotten bigger," he announced, and set the rat on a blond girl's head. The girl screamed and the week went downhill from there.

Thursday was a field trip, already arranged by the departed biologist. There was no money to charter a bus, so Eril had been left instructions to walk the children to the corner and catch the 16B Ypsilanti/Ann Arbor to the Natural History Museum. The docent delivered the museum rules while standing next to a transparent plastic woman with light-up organs. Bored, the children pressed the buttons to light her pancreas, large intestine, esophagus. Then the boys figured out what the mammary glands were, and the woman lit up like a strobe light, like a showgirl, until the bulb in her left breast went out with a loud snap. A hot, burning smell lingered.

"They're very immature," a voice commented, down by Eril's waist. She looked down at Donald's brown hair, so light it looked dusty, like he was either prematurely old or extremely dirty. He'd worn a sweatshirt with dinosaurs on it to mark the occasion. He'd said it like that, "to mark the occasion."

"Maybe you should tell them to stop."

"They'll get bored in a minute."

"You're the teacher. You should tell them to stop."

"You should mind your own business."

"You're not a very good teacher, are you?"

"Maybe you're not a very good student."

"That's not true," Donald said. "I'm an excellent student."

Of Eril's twenty students, she'd decided she liked Donald the least. He'd held her hand on the bus, refusing to notice the way the other kids mocked him, and lectured her on how Archaeopteryx was the first prehistoric bird with both scales and feathers, and how during the Ice Age Mastodons had once walked here, right here, along the 16B bus route. It seemed to Eril that there was something very wrong with him.

The docent walked them past the plastic woman to the Hall of Dinosaurs and paused by a duck-billed Parasaurolophus skull. "Are you signed up for the planetarium show?" she asked Eril.

"Sure," Eril said. "The planetarium sounds good."

"They might be a little young."

"For the planetarium? They'll be okay."

During the show a cartoon astronaut, white and puffy like the Michelin Man, floated across the starry ceiling. "The surface of the sun is very hot," the narrator intoned. "Much too hot for humans to survive. They would burn up instantly." The astronaut disappeared into the yellow circle of the sun as a man's screams faded into silence on the soundtrack. One of the students whimpered. On the way back to Morningcroft, Eril threatened not to let the troublemakers, the mammary gland boys, the whimpering girl, the incessantly chatty Donald, back on the bus. "I'm going to leave you here," she said. "Let's see how you like that." It was a clumsy threat, Eril knew as she made it. The kids knew she didn't mean it, and this just confirmed what they'd suspected for a week: Ms. Larcom was not a very good teacher.

At the staff meeting that afternoon Eril asked about curriculum, about lesson plans, about discipline, about what was and was not appropriate for third graders, about all the things she was only just realizing she knew absolutely nothing about. Besides the principal and secretary there were four other teachers, refugees who had come to Morningcroft Montessori in search of a place to exercise their frustrated talents, their curricula reflecting the different directions they wished their lives had taken. One decorated bulletin boards with her own hand-painted borders, spent two weeks every January on watercolor reproductions of famous paintings, the originals taped to the students' desks so they could be confronted with their own inadequacy. Another recycled the vocabulary of modern dance into stress-relieving activities, physical fitness initiatives. The fifth-grade teacher had filled her classroom with all the musical instruments she could afford, meaning mostly bongos and plastic xylophones. She had written a version of the Code of Hammurabi set to bongo accompaniment for a unit on Justice Through the Ages. "*An eye for an eye, a tooth for a tooth*," she sang, drumming her hands on the table. "The kids love it."

They asked Eril what drove her, what she loved, what she could twist into thematic units that met MEA standards for the third-grade year. But Eril was a woman without great talents, forced to pride herself on small, unexpected skills, like the way she could untangle knots, hold her breath for two and a half minutes, or the way she'd taught herself in the sixth grade to balance things on her head the way women did in third-world countries or finishing schools. She still practiced sometimes, unloading groceries from the car and balancing a twelve-pack of diet soda on the top of her head, plastic bags in each hand.

That Friday, the end of her first week, Eril commenced teaching grammar. It was something she knew. The four types of conditionals, starting with the Zero. The conditional tense for certitude, a state of inevitability: *If you heat water to 100 degrees Celsius, it boils,* Eril wrote, then crossed it out. *If students misbehave, they are punished,* she wrote in larger letters. The chalk squeaked as she made the final *d* and the children complained. Eril rapped her knuckles on the board. "Five examples in your notebooks. Go."

She walked around the room and looked over their shoulders. *If you go to the sun, you die. If astronauts go to a star, they scream and burn up.* Donald had two sentences so far: *If climate change happens, species go extinct,* and *If people are mean to someone, they will be sorry.*

"That's the first conditional," Eril said. "We haven't learned that yet."

"They *are* sorry," Donald corrected.

"It's grammatically correct. But it's not really true. They aren't usually sorry at all, are they?"

Donald erased his sentence.

Morningcroft was not a real Montessori school. Morningcroft was not, as far as Eril could tell, a real anything apart from some last-ditch effort to avoid Ypsilanti public schools. For parents who couldn't afford other private schools or charters and didn't bother looking too closely, there was always Morningcroft. The student body, Steckelberg had told her, was a stimulating combination of disadvantaged youth and wealthy hippie offspring. Eril had just earned an Associate's Degree in Behavioral Science at Washtenaw Community College. She'd switched from a Hospitality major in her last semester; a surprising number of the requirements had been the same.

When Eril saw her friends all they wanted to talk about was the job, how funny it was, Eril as a schoolteacher, Eril who'd never cared for school, who couldn't do math, who had no affection for English beyond the mechanics of it, who, at twenty-one, hadn't even scraped through a real college, who had filled out applications to be a desk clerk at the Marriott, an assistant manager at a sandwich shop, a receptionist at a furniture distributor, and a schoolteacher, and gotten hired by the school. "It's just for the semester," she told them. "Teaching's not for me."

"We could have told you that," they said, and she'd wish desperately that someone had.

On her better days, she could decide it wouldn't have made any difference if they had or hadn't. As little as Morningcroft could get away with paying her, without certification, without a clue, it was more than she'd earn elsewhere. Enough to keep her in her apartment, pay the higher car insurance premiums since her parents had removed themselves as co-drivers. Enough to call her parents and give them the number of a cell phone she'd paid for herself.

On other days Eril would drive the long route home, back into Ann Arbor, past the house she'd grown up in and that her parents had sold, and think about how she could teach forever and never afford to live in that neighborhood again. She felt as if the job, her whole post-parent life, was an elaborate game with particular rules about money, about independence, about fortitude; it was only sometimes that she remembered there was no judge, no winner to be declared, no prize to be awarded.

One of the rat's tumors kept growing, swelling out from his armpit to the size of a Ping-Pong ball. It dragged along the ground as he walked, until there was a bald patch at the bottom of the swell. The children refused to touch him anymore. Eril followed her predecessor's instructions to the letter, but the rat got sicker, the snake got sluggish, the shells got stinkier. Whatever kind of green thumb the other woman had had with animals, Eril thought, she had the opposite. The water in the fish tank grew cloudier. There were special snails, Donald explained, who were supposed to eat the algae but couldn't keep up since Eril didn't seem to take good enough care of the water. The snails hid all day, Donald said, sleeping, but if it was dark and quiet, like at night, they would come out and start eating the algae. This, he told Eril and the rest of the class, was called *nocturnal*.

"I know that," she said, and wrote it on the board with a line under it.

Donald asked, "Do you know what the opposite is called? What we are? Sleeping at night?"

"Why don't you tell us?"

"Maybe I don't want to."

Eril didn't know the word he meant, and Donald knew it. She turned to the blackboard. *Second Conditional,* she wrote. *If Donald behaved himself, he would not have to touch the rat.* The class whispered. Eril walked to the table, the thin floor echoing beneath her. She lifted Binx out of the cage, supporting the tumor with her right palm so the weight of it wouldn't drag on the rat's skin. She carried Binx to Donald's desk and set him down, cupping her hands into a loose enclosure. "Touch the rat," Eril ordered.

"*Diurnal.* The word was *diurnal.*"

"It's a little late for that. Touch."

Grimly Donald stroked the smooth white fur on the rat's head. The rat's whiskers twitched.

"Now touch the tumor," Eril said. That had been the Word of the Day two weeks ago, *tumor,* so the students could put a name to what was happening to their class rat, define his misfortune and use it in a sentence.

"Ewwwwww. . . ," the class called out, and Eril shushed them. For once it worked, and the classroom was silent as Donald traced the bulge with the tip of his index finger. Eril saw him shaking and almost told him to stop, it was all right, he could stop. But only almost. The class was quieter than it had been all semester. She couldn't fold now.

That night Eril's mother called to gloat about the weather. "What's the temperature there? Forty-something?" Eril's parents had sold the house just after Christmas; her father had taken early retirement, and they'd kept an eye on real estate prices, looked at condominiums in Florida or Arizona, places where they would never have to shovel snow again. The day they left for Scottsdale, Eril moved into a studio apartment filled with boxes of her old books, clothes, stuffed animals that her parents had announced they would no longer have room for. She had her bedroom furniture and whatever else her parents hadn't wanted. She had two coffee tables and no couch. She'd sit on one table, put her feet up on the other, and watch her parents' old television set. The boxes stayed piled along the walls, four of them wedged under the card table she ate at. She'd forget and bang her knees against them as she ate frozen pizza in the evening.

"I guess it's in the forties," Eril told her mother.

"You know what it's like here?"

"Nice?"

"Like you wouldn't believe. I'm sure you'll have another freeze before spring, too."

"Probably."

"How's the boyfriend?"

"There's no boyfriend. Not since August. You know that."

"That was August. Plenty of time for someone new."

"There isn't anyone." Eril curled her legs beneath her on the sturdier coffee table.

"Are you looking?"

"I'm trying not to get devoured by small children."

"The job's going that well?"

I tortured a child today, Eril wanted to say. I made a boy touch a dying rat. "The bathroom's right in my classroom, practically," she said. "Just this flimsy door. You can hear the kids peeing. It's too weird."

"I put the old amaryllis, you know, from the backyard, in the guest bathroom here but it hasn't bloomed. I don't think there's enough light."

"The kids are pretty crazy. I can't make them shut up."

"Hats off, Eril. I wouldn't teach kids. You were enough, and there was only one of you."

"I really don't know what I'm doing."

"I'm sure you're doing just fine."

"I'm really not." I should quit, she almost said. I should get out before I hit one of them. I don't know what's happening to me.

"Modesty gets you nowhere. Your father and I are both very proud of you, you know. Really showing your independence."

"Thanks," Eril said, swinging her legs out to rest them on a box behind the coffee table. Her feet sank through the top and she felt the plush fur of old stuffed animals squish beneath her toes. "That means a lot."

The next week the ground refroze into ridges and canyons of mud and weeds, footprints and tire tracks caught rigid by the cold snap and dusted with snow flurries. The kids came to school in boots again, left them at the door and went to their desks in sock feet. Eril passed out a grammar worksheet and tried to get them to work in pairs, boy-girl: it was mutiny. They shouted in protest, they howled about cooties. The biggest boy poked a girl in the eye, and Eril couldn't tell whether or not he meant to do it. The sound level in the room rose, tidal and swelling; it broke over her, and she turned to the board and wrote, Third Conditional: *If the class had listened to Ms. Larcom, they would not have had to go outside.*

"Recess!" the eye-poker said.

"No," Eril said. "This is a punishment. Get in your line."

"Boots come first," the eye-pokee reminded her. "Then line."

"No boots," Eril said, and stared them all down. It was strange, she thought, the way they didn't protest. They howled bloody murder at boys working with girls, but she could lead them like lambs out onto the frozen dirt of the yard. They stood there in a line in their socks, without coats, and she looked at each of their feet: stripey, mismatched, Spider-man, Barbie, plain white athletic. Two girls were in tights, one boy barefoot. She saw faces at the windows of the other portables and waited for someone to come outside, to tell her to stop. No one did. Finally she looked at her watch. It was almost time for math. "Back inside," she said, watching them file past, shivering. Surely they'd tell their parents, the parents would tell Steckelberg, and she'd be fired. She felt only relief.

But Steckelberg never came to talk to her. No one came,

and Eril wondered if the kind of parents who sent their kids to Morningcroft ever actually asked what they did there. Eventually the children had neat lists of sample sentences written in their notebooks, four kinds of conditionals plus mixed clauses. *If Sammy had not made farting noises, Ms. Larcom would not have taken his lunch. If Lindsey had not passed notes about Ms. Larcom in class, Ms. Larcom would not have cut a piece of her hair off. If PJ had not put a tack on Donald's seat, Ms. Larcom would not have made him sit on a tack himself to see how he liked it. If Donald weren't always such a know-it-all, Ms. Larcom would never have put masking tape over his mouth.*

The animals were getting worse, too. The fish tank was thick with algae and thicker with snails. One night Eril had worked late with only a desk lamp on, and she'd seen them emerge, inching out of their hiding places to climb up the walls, their slimy gray bodies pressed against the glass. That night, at another staff meeting where no one would meet her eyes, Eril stayed after to talk to the principal.

"It's about the animals," she said. "Something needs to be done." She explained about the death, the stink, the strange, unsettling ways they were all falling apart.

"That's good material," Steckelberg said. "The circle of life. Plan some lessons around it."

"Is that really a lesson we want them to learn? Aren't they kind of young?"

"You seem to be teaching them all kinds of lessons, Ms. Larcom. I'm really not sure why you're objecting to this one."

Eril looked at him, swallowed, tried to think of a way to explain herself. Wondered if he shouldn't be the one to explain himself, if he knew what she was doing and hadn't intervened.

"Just make it to the end of the semester, Ms. Larcom. That's all any of us are expecting. Just make it to June."

Binx made it to April 21st. Eril found him dead that morning and emptied the pencils out of a rectangular box in the supply cupboard. She lifted the bulging rat into the box and covered him with a tissue. She closed the lid, Scotch-taped it shut, and wrote "Binx" across the top. Then the students began arriving and there was no time to bury him. Before Eril could hide the box, they saw it and demanded to bury the rat themselves. Eril assigned them into groups to handle formalities like "Eulogy," "Gravesite Selection," "Hole Digging." They scheduled the funeral for after lunch. But when Eril went to pick up the coffin from the windowsill, it was gone. The children denied knowing anything. She made them drag their chairs against the wall and sit still while she searched. The box was in Donald's desk, the cardboard top open, the rat nestled inside.

"You stole my rat," Eril said, holding the box in front of Donald's face.

"The class's rat."

"Whatever. You've got a dead rat in your desk."

"I wanted to tell Binx goodbye."

"You have to ask the teacher if you can do something like that. Maybe Binx died of something catching."

There was a general shifting of bodies and thunking of chairs as the students moved away from Donald and Binx and Eril.

"The word is *contagious*," Donald said.

"You're staying inside for the funeral. Then you're staying after. We'll sit here until the snails come out."

"Fine," Donald said. Eril felt victorious, that the boy with the enormous vocabulary was reduced to "fine" in the face of her authority. Her discipline was flailing but final.

After Binx had been eulogized and buried, Donald's face at the classroom window, after a multiplication quiz and a map review, the other children packed their backpacks and went home. Eril turned off the lights and closed the shades. Donald's face was lit by the lights inside the aquarium, shining through the algae-clouded water. They sat together, close to the tank, and Eril knew she must look the same way, green and unearthly. They waited for what felt like a very long time and Eril looked behind her, realized she couldn't make out the face of the wall clock. She wondered how Donald got home, who picked him up, if there was a bus he caught, if he walked.

Hating children left her breathless. It made her feel power-less, to hate someone so small, thin, fragile people who could not even tie shoes correctly, who ate pudding snacks and played kickball and whose handwriting was clumsy, unpracticed. Who fumbled with their snow pants and seemed unable to navigate even the most basic challenges life would provide. Who, even so, would not respect her and would not listen. It took her outside of herself. Ms. Larcom was someone helpless, petty, venal. She was cruel and incompetent. She was not Eril, could not be. *Could not*: modal verb, negative certainty.

"Donald, if you need to get home—" she said, splitting the silence, the soft gurgle of the water filters. "If there's a bus you need to catch—"

"Shhhh. . . ," Donald said, and put his index finger to his lips. It was like all his gestures, studied, precise, like human behavior learned from pictures instead of from actual humans. It made her want to hit him.

"I'm not saying I don't think you need punishment. I'm just saying—"

"Shhhh, please."

"Donald, I'm saying you can go."

"The snails won't come out unless you're quiet."

"I don't care if the snails come out."

"If the snails don't come out, we can't leave." He looked at her, stricken but instructional, explaining a truth that she'd conveniently forgotten. He put one hand on his hip and the other he used to scold her, wagging his finger in the air in front of her face. In the green light he looked underwater, the pale hand floating in front of her.

"Donald, I'm sorry. Forget about the snails. You can go."

"Be quiet, please."

"I'm trying to apologize."

"Please, Ms. Larcom."

"I'm sorry about Binx. I'm sorry about everything."

"Shush, Ms. Larcom."

"Is there something I can do for you, Donald? Do you need a ride home? Tell me what you want me to do."

"Be quiet, please," Donald said, almost moaning. "Just please be quiet, or we'll never get to leave."

World Champion Cow of the Insane

They met in Bowling 101 and they would take pleasure in this, years later: that they could say they'd met in Bowling. The professor bracketed the students into miniature leagues and Robin Lerman and Charlie Brindell turned out to be the stars of Bowling 101, really quite extraordinary bowlers, the envy of the forward-thinking freshmen and last-minute seniors dispensing with the physical education requirement at Western Michigan University. Robin and Charlie were both the latter, and were already starting to think ahead to May. They resisted what was happening, this falling in love with each other in the spring of their senior year.

During a special weeknight session of Cosmic Bowling, Charlie couldn't help noticing the way Robin's white T-shirt glowed under the black light. Techno music pulsed as the pins shone off in the distance. Robin leaned toward Charlie, her ball a black hole in her hands, her T-shirt haloing around it, and asked if he wanted to go to the Henry Ford Museum with her on Saturday. "For my museum studies capstone. I have to drive to Dearborn. Do you want to come?"

"Yes," Charlie thought, and said it, "Yes."

Robin spent the two hours between Kalamazoo and Dearborn talking about a cross-country road trip she'd taken the summer before: the Barbed Wire Museum, the World's Deepest Hand-Dug

Well, the Warren G. Harding Childhood Home, the Winchester Mystery House in San Joaquin. "We stopped everywhere," she said, and Charlie resisted asking who the other half of the "we" had been.

"In Traverse City," he said. "We have the International Nun Museum. Two hundred Barbies dressed in all the habits of the world."

"You're from Traverse City?"

"Near it. Beulah." Charlie showed her where that was, his right hand spread flat, fingers together, his palm a map of Michigan's lower peninsula. He touched his own hand near the tip of the pinkie.

"Chicago," Robin said, taking her hand off the wheel to brush the left south shore of his palm, where the state line crawled down the edge of his wrist. "Are you going back, in May?"

Charlie nodded. "My dad has a construction business."

"A job. That's key, right there."

"It's paradise, too," he said. "There's always that."

At the museum, Charlie followed Robin through the classic cars and the Hall of American Inventions. They talked their way onto the assembly line in the children's area: Robin did axles while Charlie did steering wheels. The kid doing rear tires kept messing up and Charlie almost yelled; he'd wanted their wooden cars to turn out perfectly. He'd wanted to see them parked in the little lot at the end of the line and say, "We made all those."

They stayed until closing, ate dinner at a shawarma place and then went for a beer. Neither wanted to drive back to Kalamazoo, and so they decided to spend the night at a hotel, buy a six-pack. "Beulah," Robin sang, sprawling on the bed with her toes against the headboard. Charlie turned on HBO, just to try and get their money's worth out of the room. "It sounds like a country song. *I lost my dog in Beulah,*" Robin yodeled.

"Don't knock it 'til you've seen it," Charlie said. "We've got the World Champion Cow of the Insane."

"An insane champion cow?"

"The world champion cow *of* the insane."

"What the hell is that?"

"I guess you'll have to go up north to find out. You'll just have to come up north with me," Charlie said, and finally kissed her.

Robin would think, years later, that couples should never honeymoon anywhere they might someday live. The comparison wouldn't do anyone any favors. Don't shit where you eat and don't vacation where it could be you renting out the Ski-Doos next season. She would think that too much happiness, too early, made a person distrustful. She would think that watching too many sunsets over water could spoil a person, that too much summer poisoned the winter after. That summer, though, the summer she and Charlie Brindell were both twenty-two and very much in love, the rule never occurred to her. Charlie was from paradise, he'd grown up in paradise, and he'd brought her there to share in it. They had known each other for sixteen weeks, spent eight of those as no more than bowling rivals. Now they worried that they had fallen blindsidingly, gobsmackingly in love with each other. Charlie had called his mother to tell her about Robin two weeks before graduation, and she had asked if she should make up both bunks in his childhood bedroom when he came home for the summer. Upon being reminded that he was a man who still slept in a bunk bed, Charlie tried to convince himself that he was too young to be in love with anyone. He was much too young to be *sure*.

Brindell Builders had a contract renovating ancient resort cottages built four-deep on narrow lots surrounding Empire Lake, twenty-five miles inland from Lake Michigan. Charlie's father looked the other way when Robin and his son moved into a frontage cabin as soon as the plumbing was hooked up. Charlie brought home flowers Robin put in Mason jars; she made him eggs in the mornings, learned how to use a level and a power saw. They spent weekend days at the beach, and watched the Cherry Princess crowned at the Cherry Harvest Parade. They did the dune climb at the national park, and took photographs of Sleeping Bear itself, the dune that was eroding, that would slide, the rangers told them, off the bluff and into Lake Michigan within a generation. They visited the International Nun Museum, and Robin bought a set of magnets. She bought old posters at the flea market in Weldon to tack to the bare walls of their borrowed home, and little beeswax soaps from a beekeeper in Benzonia. That summer, their bodies smelled like honey, and they could lie in bed under the ceiling fan and press their noses against each other's skin and smell the slow scent of sated bees in a field near the Benzie River.

Charlie was blond and tan to his waist, the burnt brown-over-red of a pale man who works outdoors. Robin would lay her hand against his chest and worry he'd get skin cancer someday. Then she'd picture them as two old people, lovingly cancerous together in a little house on a lake somewhere. Robin's father was black, her mother white, and Robin what her parents had joked was the warm color of an expensive coffee drink, her hair dark and tightly curled. Elderly Latina women had always come up to her asking for directions. *I'm not Dominican,* she'd tell them, in English. *No, not Puerto Rican. I don't even speak Spanish.* In Chicago, or even Kalamazoo, Robin hadn't stood out. In Beulah, Robin would watch people watch her, not hostile, just curious, wondering, *What are you? Are you—something? Something different than what we are?*

What are you? Robin was always tempted to ask them. *What somethings are all of you?*

During weekdays Charlie worked for his father and Robin volunteered at the Museum of Maritime Rescue; if she got her foot in the door, her supervisor had said, the Park Service might have something for her next summer. She retyped the labels for an exhibit about knots and gave presentations to visiting groups of summer campers. She spread a blue tarpaulin on the grass behind the museum and asked for volunteers to step onto it. The cut-ups waved their arms around and shrieked for help as Robin tossed ropes that slapped dryly against their sneakers.

On Sunday mornings Robin and Charlie went to Leland and looked at the boats in the slips. It was like touring a zoo, the habitats and lifestyles of the rich and aquatic, the white boats filled with tanned women in Capri pants and broad sunhats. Men in cargo shorts and polo shirts would come up the steps from the galley with trays of yellow eggs, blackened toast, rose-colored bacon, orange juice and champagne in long-stemmed glasses. Even the children were angular and bright, spidering around the confines of the fifteen-foot *Easy Street,* out of Manistee, or the thirty-foot *Lazy Daze,* out of Port Huron, or the enormous two-story *Sunny Side,* out of Grand Haven, whose dining deck stood well above the pier and which Robin and Charlie knew only from the enormous laughter that floated over the starboard side, the glimpses of dangling feet and hands and wet towels flapping from the railings. They all looked like people in advertisements for summer clothes, for boats, towels, lakes, a state of being.

The older women had small, soft white dogs. Once a Shih Tzu jumped from the stern of a boat onto the pier and circled Robin's ankles, confused, its toenails catching on the rubber strap of her flip-flops. Charlie scooped the dog into his arms as its owner climbed out to meet them. She offered them a drink. In the flaring red sunset they toasted Charlie's dog-catching abilities. Robin raised her glass and watched the light pour across the water through the clear vodka tonic. The waves slapped against the hull and Robin felt the deck rock beneath her. Her life, she thought, would be large with joy.

Brindell Builders finished the Empire Lake job after Labor Day and Mr. Brindell gently evicted Robin and Charlie. Robin rolled up the posters, stripped the bed, put the last of the honey soap in a Ziploc bag and spent three weeks on Charlie's top bunk. "I think it's time I got a job," she told him.

But it was October: the fudge shops were closed, the kayak rentals shuttered, the boats in Leland going into dry dock. A strip club called the Pirate's Booty didn't need any more servers.

"We don't need any more performers, either," they added.

"I wasn't asking," Robin said.

The Beulah Community Center needed someone for six hours a week to teach classes on basic Internet usage. The Educational Outreach Coordinator, Mrs. Halstead, was a grandmotherly woman who had once babysat for Charlie. She called Robin "Honey" and was straightforward about the prospects. "Retirees wanting to open email attachments with pictures of their grandkids. Maybe sell stuff on eBay," she explained. "That'd be about it, Honey."

Robin taught Tuesday and Thursday mornings, never more

than three or four people in each class. Tuesday's only attendee was Mr. Zendler, frail and spotted, with the beginnings of a hump rising above his bent head. Robin instructed him in the finer points of a free email account. "Click on 'Compose Message,' right here," she said, pointing to the screen with a long pink pipe cleaner she'd found in the Center's Arts & Crafts closet. Mr. Zendler had brought his son's email address written on a folded paper napkin, and Robin watched him hunt-and-peck it in. "Then the subject line."

"Y-o-u a-r-e a m-o-t-h-e-r-f-u-c-k-i-n-g i-g-n-o-r-a-m-u-s," Mr. Zendler spelled out, painstakingly, on the keyboard.

"Just so you know, I don't think a subject line that long will show up in his inbox."

Mr. Zendler backspaced his way to "Fucking Ignoramus = YOU."

"Is there anything going on I should know about?" Robin asked.

"That *you* should know about?" Mr. Zendler snorted. Actually snorted, and Robin went home that night and told Charlie, "This old guy snorted at me today."

He was back on Thursday. Twenty minutes into the class he left the computer lab and came back with red plastic lunch trays from the kitchen. He built little walls around his computer and glared at the rest of the class. It was clearly an effort for him, reaching to position and balance the trays. Robin wanted for a moment to help him. She had written her email address on the whiteboard, so the seniors could send practice messages, and after class was over and she'd put the trays back she checked her account. Subj: Snoop = YOU! from Joseph.Zendler@hotmail.com.

> Dear Miss Lerman,
> You are a good teacher except for when you are trying to read my personal correspondences over my shoulder so I ask you to please stop thank you very much.
> Sincerely,
> Mr. Joseph Zendler
> PS—Where are you from? Detroit?

Sorry, Mr. Zendler. I wasn't trying to read your email. I just hope, that if there are family problems, you'll talk to someone at the Community Center about it. Please let me know if you need help with anything.
Best wishes,
Robin Lerman
PS—I am not from Detroit.

On one of the last nice afternoons of the year, Robin and Charlie visited the old state mental hospital, an enormous complex of Tudor-style stone palaces, decommissioned and emptied of patients. One wing was a bed and breakfast; the staff quarters had gone condo. The old lobby was a museum, featuring a glass display case of Items Ingested by Mental Patients: a buffalo nickel, a shoelace, a strip of film, most of a light bulb, the sleeve of an old Coast Guard-issue raincoat. Robin and Charlie had mugs of hot cider in a cafeteria with bars across the windows, then walked around the grounds, yellow grass and bare trees. They held hands inside a wide pocket of Charlie's coat. Under an oak an enormous gravestone marked the resting place of the World Champion Cow of the Insane.

"You didn't tell me she was dead."

"Only blue-ribbon milk cow ever tended solely by the mentally deficient. Don't let anyone tell you there's nothing to do in Benzie County," Charlie said.

In class the next week Mr. Zendler was in a confiding mood. "My son's trying to get me to move downstate," he said, after the other seniors had left. "Says I shouldn't be up in the woods alone."

"How far out do you live?"

"In the park. The access road's seasonal, but I've got chains."

"*In* the park? Sleeping Bear?"

"The government bought this whole county for nothing. They bought just enough so the rest of us couldn't afford taxes and couldn't sell to anyone but them. A handful of us wouldn't budge, got our property grandfathered in."

"You're living by yourself in the national park?"

"I just *said* that. And I've got a *house.* I'm not living in a tent like a goddamn hippie or something."

"But is that safe?"

"Last time I tell you anything."

"Okay, sorry. But just—let me know if you ever need help with anything."

"You can bring me some groceries after class."

"You came around fast."

"Pretty girl offers to bring me things, how do I refuse? I'll type a list. Make a map in that drawing program. Send them as email attachments. Last time I checked I was supposed to be learning something in here."

The next afternoon Robin took Charlie's pickup to the grocery store with Mr. Zendler's list and followed his directions deep into the park. She turned off onto a restricted access road, the pickup churning on fresh snow. The house was several miles in, a peeling A-frame sitting in a clearing where the road dead-ended. Mr. Zendler didn't help her carry his groceries in, but he did make them both tea, one bag for two cups. He insisted she take her coat off, warm her hands over the space heater he'd dragged alongside the kitchen table. The room was spare, bare walls and linoleum flooring. A handful of magnets were stuck to the fridge—a calendar from an insurance agent, a baby picture in a hard plastic sleeve, a cutout of a Ski-Doo. The only clutter was a mountain of black trash bags piled in a corner of the kitchen. The smell was ferocious, seeping into the tea until Robin pushed her mug away. "Do you mind taking away some garbage with you?" Mr. Zendler asked. "Don't exactly get curbside pickup out here."

Robin shrugged. "Okay."

"You seem like a great girl, Robin."

"Thanks."

"You deserve a good man."

"Mr. Zendler—"

"I don't mean me, ignoramus. I'm 82 years old."

"I've already got a good guy."

"You need a better one."

"I have Charlie Brindell. Do you know him? Does he pass inspection?"

"Sure, I know Charlie. Like I said, you deserve a better one."

"What's that supposed to mean?"

"Nothing you won't find out in due time, Honey."

"Mr. Zendler—"

"I'm afraid I'm feeling like I need a rest. Take your time, leave when you're ready. And thanks for taking that trash with you." Mr. Zendler disappeared into a room off the front hall and shut the door. Robin stood by herself in the kitchen, then started dragging trash bags, heaving them into the truck bed. Bag by bag, she moved the mountain out of Mr. Zendler's house.

Robin and Charlie had found an apartment to rent, a one-bedroom unit in a resort-owned complex on Lake Mullett, smaller than Empire, a little farther inland. Mr. Brindell had helped them negotiate a special rate for the off-season. They didn't know where they'd live come summer. Robin put the posters back up, used the honey soap down to damp splinters. The night after she visited Mr. Zendler she boiled frozen ravioli and over dinner asked where they could dump a truckload of garbage bags.

"The landfill, but we'd have to pay," Charlie said.

"I couldn't just let them sit there."

"Zendler's not your problem. He's been around forever. My dad worked on his house when he was trying to get enough built to hold onto the claim."

"Is there a reason you don't want me helping him?" Robin asked, and Charlie looked confused. In bed that night they squeezed together to sleep, pressing skin to skin for the warmth of it. The next morning Charlie woke up and said, "I dreamed I loved you and you didn't love me back."

"Don't dream that," she said.

"I can't help what I dream."

Mr. Zendler didn't show up to the next class until nearly the end. He sat quietly at the far side of the computer lab, typing an email that turned out to be for her.

> Dear Miss Lerman,
> Like I said, we all know each other around here and you are new to the County and I should tell you that you don't know everything there is to know about Charlie Brindell. You should WATCH OUT!
> Sincerely,
> Joseph Zendler (Your Student)

The Museum of Maritime Rescue was closed for the season, but Robin had continued to volunteer in the afternoons, doing exhibit maintenance, some filing and envelope-stuffing. She drove home in the dark. It had been snowing off and on all that week and the roads were soaked in brown slush. The truck surfed when Robin braked. She was glad for the garbage still in the truck bed, keeping her from fishtailing too badly. "You seduced me," she told Charlie when she got home.

"I hope so."

"No, you seduced me with the World Champion Cow of the Insane. With the Cherry Parade. I didn't know it was going to be like this."

"Like what?"

"Look around."

"What?"

"If you don't know, I don't know how to tell you."

"There's the Humongous Fungus Fest next summer," Charlie offered. "The World's Largest Fungus is in the upper peninsula."

"I've fallen for that before," Robin told him.

There was an email every day now from Mr. Zendler, for a week straight:

> Brindell Builders cheats everyone in town. They are cheats and Jews and the whole town knows it. Charlie can't hammer a nail in straight. Why do you think they only work for the big resorts with out-of-state owners?
> You think he is your great boyfriend, but you don't know what he does when you are not around. You have no idea.

Charlie Brindell is sleeping with all the WHORES in town. That makes you a WHORE too. Even if you're a nice girl that makes you a whore Internet teacher person.

Do you know where Charlie was last night? Why can't you keep your husband happy?

Robin did know: last night she and Charlie had watched *Law & Order* and played gin rummy. But even this could not entirely dissipate the threat of Mr. Zendler's message.

"I looked up the Humongous Fungus Fest," Robin offered. An ice storm had taken out the electricity during *CSI,* and Charlie was lighting candles. "It's underground. The fungus."

"Oh," Charlie said. "I just always pictured a giant mushroom. I've never actually been."

"Armillaria Bulbosa, thirty-seven acres. You know what the featured events are?"

Charlie shrugged, his shape outlined by a votive candle he'd lit in an empty jar.

"A cribbage tournament, pie social, and Finn vs. Polack softball game."

"I'd have thought that's up your alley. You liked the nun museum."

"Finn vs. Polack softball? I have my limits, Charlie. You don't know me at all."

Robin printed out copies of the emails and made an appointment to speak with Mrs. Halstead. They met in her office, a wood-paneled room in the community center basement, a narrow rectangular window at the top of the wall almost flush with the parking lot outside. Mrs. Halstead was horrified.

"We'll get him out of the class before tomorrow," she said. "I'll talk to him. Maybe have my husband give him a call. There are people he still listens to. Honey, why did you wait so long?"

"You don't have to throw him out of the class, really. I want him to have the opportunity to learn—if he needs to get hold of his son sometime, or—"

"Honey, he's been coming to these classes since they started. If he's been playing dumb, well, he's been playing."

Robin paused. "Still. I didn't come to you to—to have him thrown out."

"Then you came to what? Because these emails are entirely unacceptable."

"I wanted—" Robin found she couldn't say it, and trailed off, the pink pipe cleaner she used as a screen-pointer bent around her fingers. Outside the thin basement window the snow was patchy and ugly, the parking lot covered in gravel and salt.

"You want to know if it's true."

Robin nodded, realizing as she did that she didn't trust herself to speak. Her throat felt tight and stretched, how she imagined swallowing the sleeve of a raincoat felt, the glass and metal cuff of a light bulb.

"Oh, Honey. Honey. Mr. Zendler is crazy. He's holed up out there in the park by himself, and I know he looks awfully frail, but he's crazy as a loon. He hates the summer people. He hates the new people. The police have hauled him in for booby-trapping the woods. He put up tripwires across snowmobile paths. Someone could have been killed."

"So he doesn't—"

"He hates everyone, really. He's been banned from the Pirate's Booty for harassing the girls. Someone told me he'd been banned from the Elks' Bingo game for trying to cheat."

"He doesn't—know anything, about Charlie?"

"I've known Charlie since he was six years old. Has he given you any reason—"

"No, I just—"

"Then Good Lord, stop looking for one. Charlie's a good boy. And if you believe this nonsense over—"

"I'm sorry, okay? I'm sorry. No one told me Mr. Zendler was batshit insane, okay?" Robin jerked up out of the plastic chair Mrs. Halstead had offered her. "How would I know that? How would I know you all knew?"

"Sit down, Honey."

Robin fell back into the chair, bent at the waist with her arms wrapped around her stomach.

"You couldn't. I suppose you couldn't."

Robin leaned her forehead against the edge of the desk, and her voice floated back up to Mrs. Halstead from the floor. "I feel really stupid now."

"Don't. I'm sorry I didn't know what was happening."

"You won't tell him?" Robin asked, turning her head so her cheek was resting on the table, her eyes looking up at Mrs. Halstead.

"Charlie?"

Robin nodded, her head still pressed against the desk.

"No, I won't tell him."

"Thank you."

"No need, Honey. No need."

"This weekend," Charlie said that night over Scrabble, "I thought we could maybe get out of town. Go south to visit your parents. Stop in Battle Creek and go to Cereal City, or this Historic Seventh-Day Adventists Village I read about. Since the Fungus Fest sounds like it isn't worth waiting for."

"I don't hate it here, Charlie."

Charlie didn't say anything, just put down his tiles. He made H-I-T-S and Robin wanted to tell him, No, save the S for later. Add it to something with an X or Z. "I don't hate it here. I want to be here with you. I'd sell saltwater taffy at the Salty Dawg's in Wharftown all summer, okay? I'd re-apply at the Pirate's Booty."

"You don't have to do that. My dad said you're the steadiest girl he's ever seen with a nail gun. You can work for him again next summer, if you want."

"I'm just saying I want to be here with you. I'm in love with you, and I just want to make that clear."

"Okay. I'm in love with you, too. And I'd like to take you to Cereal City."

"I went as a kid. You have to wear hairnets. But I could never pass up a Historic Adventist Village."

"They have costumed re-enactors who lead singalongs."

"Of what? '99 Bottles of Beer on the Wall'?"

"Nineteenth-century hymns."

"You *have* been holding out on me."

"We can leave Saturday morning," Charlie said, and Robin pictured them throwing their backpacks behind the seats in Charlie's pickup. She'd hosed out the bed after taking Mr. Zendler's garbage to the dump, and the water had frozen in a sheet of cloudy ice across the bottom of the truck, pine needles and leaves caught in the flood and freeze. They'd drive to the Historic Adventist Village in Battle Creek, and try on buckle shoes and goofy hats and bonnets, and they would sit on the hard wooden pews of a re-created clapboard church, and they would sing *Happy Day, Happy Day,* and there would be no doubt in her mind that it was so.

Steal Small

I live in a good house now, with an attic where the roof makes a triangle and the heat collects. I stand up there and look out back to the barbed wire where our property meets the neighbor's, and past that the highway. The neighbor still farms, soy planted right up against the fence. We haven't planted anything, unless you count the animals. That's what Leo does, what he grows. From the attic you can see the kennels laid out in a half circle in the backyard, all figured so the mean ones don't fight, the sweet ones calm the fussy ones down, and the bitches can't get puppies. Leo can hold them all in his head, who needs what and eats what and is looking sick and should probably be sold on before it looks any sicker. He's got a good mind for organization. I've got a good mind for keeping stuff tidy, which is important in a house like this, which is big and decent and full of what a person needs, but has fifteen dogs caged up in the back. Fifteen give or take. In a good month, take.

Leo got a real nasty scratch about a month ago, spiraling from the back of his hand down the inside of his arm. I had him sit on the bathroom counter while I got alcohol and cotton balls out of the cupboard. I dabbed my way down his arm. "Second time this week," I said. "You should watch yourself better."

"It wasn't the rottie," he said, looking up, and I couldn't tell whether or not he liked what I'd done to the ceiling. It's light blue now, with clouds. I did the clouds with a can of white paint and more cotton balls, more dabbing.

"If it wasn't the rottie—"

"One of the cage doors. I need to go back out with the wire cutters."

"You need one of those shots?"

"Tetanus? I'm fine," he said, but there's no way of knowing with Leo if he meant fine because he'd had one or fine because fine's what you are when you don't think too much about yourself, about how you're really doing and what you really need. We're both of us fine most of the time.

I was long done with the alcohol, but I was standing between Leo's legs and he'd put his feet together behind me, up against the backs of my thighs. I still had his left hand in mine. I brushed the backs of his knuckles. "The gangrene's back," he said, which it was, but he doesn't need to warn me like he thinks he does. He doesn't really have gangrene, just some weird skin thing that makes him itch so bad he scratches even in his sleep, until the skin breaks open and starts oozing, sometimes blood and sometimes something clear and sometimes both together, so his skin shines in the light like a pink glaze, like glass or pastry. He always warns me, before I uncover an elbow, or the back of a knee, or lift his shirt to find a patch on his belly. I kissed the back of his hand, a clear part, close to his wrist. His legs dropped down and he let me go, his heels kicking the cupboard doors.

"I'll go start dinner," I said.

"I'll be back in soon," he said, and hopped down off the counter. He's much taller than me, long like a noodle and skinny in his jeans. His hair's long but not too long, tied back and never greasy. He's got a Cheshire cat inked on his left front forearm. The tattoo seems to keep away the gangrene, and he jokes that he's going to save up, become the Illustrated Man, stop selling dogs at the Pick-n-Trades and just sell tickets for people to see him in his shorts.

For dinner I broiled some frozen fish, microwaved some frozen peas, baked a couple of potatoes. The window over the sink faces the back, and Leo had the dunk tank out. I guess you're supposed to spray flea stuff around the kennels, air them out with no dogs inside, but we're almost full up until the Pick-n-Trade in Joplin, and there's nowhere to move the dogs to. So he took them one by one out of the kennels and dumped them in the tank, pyrethrum insecticide mixed with water, strong enough to keep the fleas off them until market. It's bad for their eyes and skin, worse for their tempers, but Class B dealers don't mind with temperament. Leo had gloves on, a pair he stole from the outfitter's offices at the slaughterhouse, but the Rottweiler might have gotten him anyway. We've had her here for a month, since Leo found her in the Lamar classifieds and went to pick her up. I think she's homesick.

The fish didn't taste like much, but Leo's always gracious. "Where'd you learn this one?" he asks. "How'd you make that?" I sewed two buttons back onto a shirt of his the other day, which doesn't take more than a needle and a pair of eyes, but he acted like he'd seen a miracle. Did my mother sew, he asked, had she taught me, and I wanted to laugh but then he'd ask what was funny. It wasn't something my mom would care about, the way other people looked in their clothes. When Mouse got boobs I was the one who had to tell her that she needed a bra. The elastic had gone out of my old ones, but I could drive by then so we went to Wal-Mart and charged some things. It was a nice afternoon, doing that together.

Mouse lives in St. Louis now. She's going to college, studying biology. She sends me postcards, always of the Arch, the Mississippi River, things I already know how they look like. I'd like to see her campus, the streets where she lives, but she's never volunteered. She says she has a boyfriend who's studying business, and I thought about writing back how Leo has a business, too, but then she'd ask selling what. *Lyssa,* she writes. *Mango of my eye and possum of my heart. How goes it? I took summer term classes so I've got more finals already. I don't think I'll be able to make it for a visit. How's what's-his-face? It's cold and rainy in St. Louis. Hope the weather's better in Neosho. Love and Squalor, Mouse.* She always signs the postcards *Love and Squalor,* and I know it's a joke, but I don't get what's funny.

Leo only bunches part time. He works days over at National Beef. He's one of the top guys there who's not management, a twelve-dollar-an-hour man. He started off down the chain, but now he's a knocker. He stands up on the catwalk with a bolt gun and lets the cows have it as they come down the chute. "Pow, right between the eyes," he told me. He talks big but I don't think he enjoys it all that much. He stands eight hours in his rubber coverall, goggles, his hair tied back and stuffed under a net. The slaughterhouse has been losing money so steady they've got the line speed up to a cow every nine seconds, trying to do in volume what they can't do in beef prices. Down the chute and up by the ankles, Leo's quick hand on the bolt gun the only thing saving the cows from being butchered alive. "Goddamn angel of mercy," Leo says. "What kind of a life does a cow have, anyway?" He says top line speed is 400 an hour, which means Leo can kill 3,200 animals in a day, minus his breaks, two fifteen-minute ones and a half hour for lunch.

I work twenty hours a week at the Goodwill, mostly sorting donations. I'd work more if they had the hours for me. It's nasty work in lots of little ways, but since Leo's work is what it is, I can't complain to him. We have to keep the stuffed toys wrapped in plastic for two weeks in the back, to suffocate any lice that might be on them. We have to check the clothes for stains, like old blood the color of sweet potatoes on the insides of women's pants. If the clothes are stained too bad to sell, they're shipped out in big bundles to somewhere else, somewhere in Africa or South America or something.

Leo ate his potato last, scooping out the halves and then rolling the skins up into tubes with salt and pepper inside. He ate the tubes with his hands, like brown paper hot dogs. I got out ice cream bowls, a half gallon of vanilla and the kind of chocolate sauce that hardens on top of the ice cream. "I'm glad it wasn't the rottie," I said, "who scratched you. She's a pretty one."

"Pretty ugly. She's a dog."

"All your pretty uglies."

"You too, Miss Lyss. You can be my favorite. My prettiest ugly."

I tapped my spoon against the hard chocolate. Underneath the shell my ice cream was already melting.

"I'm just kidding," Leo said.

"Stop messing with the gangrene. You'll make it worse." He was rubbing his knuckles up and down on the edge of the table. When he's itching bad he'll rub his fingers against stuff without even realizing and the skin breaks open right away. There are little smears of blood all over the house, on the prickly surfaces that feel best when he's itching—the rough carpet in the rec room, the weave of the couch, the furry cover on the toilet. I could track him through the house like that, like a hurt animal, something leaking and in pain.

"Maybe it *is* worse this time. Maybe I have leprosy. My nose'll fall off. Then I'll be *your* pretty ugly."

"If your nose falls off you're not going to be my anything," I said, which sounded kind of mean, and I thought about telling him the truth, which is that he'd be my lovely ugly even if his nose did fall off, and then that seemed pathetic, and I thought perhaps I shouldn't say anything at all, so I didn't.

"If you're not working tomorrow, can you come with me?" he asked.

"Carthage?"

"Webb City."

"You got a paper?"

"We can pick one up there. Look through it over some breakfast. We'll go to the Denny's off 71."

"Sure," I said, and hoped he didn't think the Denny's was what swayed me. I don't do what I do for Leo so he'll buy me breakfast.

In bed that night I was careful of the gangrene. Leo fell asleep right after but it took me a while. It had been dark for hours, but the weather wasn't cooling. We had the ceiling fan going and the windows open. The crickets were chirping the way they did all summer, a long low buzz like power lines, and the dogs were suffering in the heat. I bet Leo'd never find anyone else who can listen to dogs cry the way I can. They call out and I can turn over and not hear them, not even a bit. I don't need the radio or the TV. I just need my own two ears and then I don't hear a thing. I dreamed good dreams but I don't remember what they were.

At Denny's, Leo got the Grand Slam and I got waffles. He took the classifieds from the *Webb City Gazette* and let me have everything else. I read about a meth lab bust and a church swap sale on the front page while Leo circled ads with a red pen. I grew up in Webb City, but with Mouse in St. Louis, there's not much to bring me back. I don't know where my mom's got to these days.

"Anything promising?"

"Loads. Some purebreds, too. Or so they're claiming. I thought we'd try and hit those first."

"Sounds fine." I went to check my hair and makeup in the bathroom while Leo settled up. I was wearing a flowered dress and sandals, my hair down, a little liner for my eyes and color for my lips, not too much. Like a Sunday School teacher, Leo said, and it was strange to hear something like that come out of him as a compliment. Leo was wearing khaki pants and a long-sleeved shirt that covered his tattoo but was too hot for the weather. He already had sweat stains under his arms. We sat in the van with the air conditioning on while Leo started calling houses on his cell phone. Beagles are good finds. Hounds, labs, retrievers, too, either purebred or close enough so you can tell the breed without squinting. It's because they're mid-sized dogs with large chest cavities, the way Leo explains it. I don't quite know why that's important but I guess it makes them easy to work with.

Before I moved in with Leo the biggest thing I'd ever stolen was a stick of butter. Not even a package, a single stick. Mouse and I had decided we wanted to make chocolate chip cookies. We found a recipe on an index card in the kitchen, but none of the ingredients. All we needed was a teaspoon of this, a half-teaspoon of that, and we didn't have anything. 1/8th of a teaspoon baking soda. We looked at the tiny bowl of the measuring spoon, the size of the nail on Mouse's pinky finger. We found a chain of little plastic snap-off paint tubs that had come with a paint-by-number set, and cleaned them out and put them in Mouse's pink vinyl purse. At the grocery store we took baking soda and baking powder off the shelf, looked both ways for clerks, opened the containers, and tapped out a few spoonfuls into the tubs. We were doing the same thing with a tin of cinnamon in the spice aisle when a woman confronted us, a lady with a cart full of food like kids would eat, fruit snacks and Hi-C. "What do you girls think you're doing?" she asked.

"We want to make cookies," Mouse said.

"Are you going to pay for that?"

"We can't. So we're only taking a little," I said, and Mouse nodded solemnly, because Mouse was already an expert in solemn truths.

The woman looked at us in our old shorts and stained T-shirts and you could watch her feeling sorry for us, deciding to let us keep right on stealing. I let Mouse put two eggs and the stick of butter in her purse after she promised to be careful with them. At the checkout we paid for flour and sugar and chocolate chips and asked for two plastic bags. I put them on the handlebars of my bike, one on each side, because I figured Mouse had enough to worry about with the eggs in her purse.

The next morning, Mouse and I were eating some of our cookies for breakfast when Mom came home. "Where'd you get cookies?" she asked, and we told her, because we figured she either wouldn't care or would think we were resourceful. She put some bread in the toaster and opened the fridge. "Where's the butter?" she asked.

"There isn't any."

"You don't put four sticks of butter in a batch of cookies."

"That's why we only took one," Mouse said.

"Lyssa and Mouse. You steal, you steal something worth taking. Then I'd at least have butter for the damn toast."

That's one of the only pieces of advice Mouse and I can remember getting from her, and I didn't even take it. I still steal small. Not things other people want, or things that are worth a lot. I just take what I need.

The first house we went to in Webb City was in my old neighborhood, a street that had been kept up a little better than the one I grew up on. The house was a nice little ranch, painted white with geraniums in the window boxes. Leo rang the doorbell and then stepped back so we were standing side by side. The woman who came to the door had an armful of brown cardboard boxes, so Leo kept it short. "Mrs. Sidore?" he said. "I called a few minutes ago. About the dog. Leo Tillet."

We were shown to the couch in the living room, which was full of boxes labeled *Estate Sale,* and *Rubbish,* and *Keep,* and *Kids Might Want???* I could feel Leo smile. Death lingers on a dog. Families want rid of it. Leo's a quick appraiser, and I knew he was looking over Mrs. Sidore and the dog she brought in, which even I could tell was a poodle, purebred or pretty close, a little gray around the muzzle but spry enough. "You're quick off the mark. The first call we've had."

"My wife and I wanted to get the jump on the Sunday ads. We've been looking for a dog and we were interested in poodles, so when we saw your ad—"

"She's purebred, from a breeder near Kansas City. I've got the American Kennel Association papers. She's been taken good care of. Shots, and spayed, although I think she's past puppies by now."

"What's her name?" Leo asked, scratching around the dog's ears until she started to wag so hard her whole butt waggled. Leo's awfully good with dogs. Good with people, too; he asked all the right questions, about health conditions, about how much exercise old Muffy needed, whether she could be let off a leash. "We have a nice piece," he said. "In the country outside of Neosho. She'd have room to run around."

"It sounds lovely," Mrs. Sidore said. "Honestly I was worried, with the dog being old, that she'd be hard to place. I don't suppose families with kids would want her, knowing she'll die and having to explain it."

"It's just my wife and I right now," Leo said. "And we don't have time to train a puppy."

"Well, Mr. Tillet, the ad was Free to a Good Home and you seem a good home and she's still free. I'll grab her papers, if you're decided, and a box of her things."

Our house is full of dog bowls, and Muffy wouldn't need toys, but Leo let Mrs. Sidore get them. I held the dog on my lap as we drove away. On the next block we stopped and Leo unlocked the back of the van. He has kennel space for six dogs back there. We locked Muffy into a cage with a dish of water and one of the toys from her box, and Leo checked the next house on his list against his map.

Leo's lucky we've got a good neighbor, by which I mean we never see each other, and never give each other any trouble. His house is on the far end of his property, and even on a clear night the sound from our yard doesn't travel. If we actually wanted to let Muffy roam free, he wouldn't say boo about it. Mouse and I, our neighbor growing up was Mr. Martin, who had a house just like ours except that ours was yellow and his was green. One summer he decided to have a big yard sale, and got all his buddies to bring over every piece of old furniture they could find, either on consignment or just to save them a trip to the dump. Offer the customers a wide selection, he kept saying, lining couches up along his driveway and across his front yard until his entire property was covered over like a furniture store, chairs in one corner, desks in another, big appliances, like an old fridge with a bright chrome handle, back by his garage. He seemed to do okay. People came and hauled some stuff away, or shook on something and promised to be back later for it. The next weekend, though, he still had half a Goodwill store spread out over his lawn. That weekend it rained, and in the morning all the furniture was soaking. Mouse and I balanced on the backs of the couches, knocking each other off onto the cushions and listening to the squelch. Pools of water rose up in perfect footprints where we stepped, and the beginnings of a smell, damp and lush, curled from the upholstery. Mr. Martin chased us off that morning, and stood for a while on his lawn, reaching his right arm over his head to scratch at the back of his neck. Mouse and I stared at the hair growing in his armpit and wondered what he'd do.

Of course, the easiest thing to do with a yard full of soaking furniture is nothing at all, and for years that's what Mr. Martin seemed settled on doing. He gave up trying to run us off, and in winter we made snow forts out of the sofas, pelted each other with secret stores of snowballs hidden under chairs and in desk drawers. After the first winter's snow melted, the smell had taken hold. The furniture was wet and moldering, the wood splitting with rot, the cushions mildewing. A pair of raccoons had started a den underneath a loveseat, and a skunk had a nest of babies under a recliner. Mouse and I would jump onto the loveseat, both together, on the count of three. When our feet pounded the springs the raccoons would shriek and shoot out. We played hide and seek and once Mouse accidentally locked herself in the old fridge, but I found her and let her out.

One family Leo and I visited that Sunday had already placed their dog. A few more were playing coy, taking our information and giving us the third degree. The fat guy with the Akita had a long list of names on a yellow legal pad, but the lady with the Bichon Frisé just wrote Leo's name and number at the top of a blank page. "I've had a few people show some interest. I'll let you know," she said, and you could tell she hadn't, but she was mighty suspicious of why a guy like Leo would want a dog like a Bichon. We picked up a chocolate Labrador from a couple who was moving to a one bedroom apartment in Kansas City in a week. An English terrier from an old woman whose family was putting her in a nursing home. She tried to serve us tea and tiny little shortbread cookies, but she dropped the cookies into the tea and didn't seem to notice. The tea was in these white china cups, and you could look down inside and see the cookie dissolving, settling in a thick layer across the bottom. The dog was skinny, with long nails, like the woman couldn't remember how to take care of it. She kissed Leo on the cheek when he took the terrier into his arms.

The summer Mouse locked herself in the fridge was the summer Mr. Martin started locking himself out of his garage. The first time it happened, Mouse was alone, playing at Boat, trying to hop as far across his yard as she could without touching the ground, which was really water and full of sharks. She'd asked me to play and I'd refused, just because I was five years older and I could, even though when we stood on chairs and rocked back and forth we moved in rhythm, without even trying, because we could feel the same waves.

"Hey, Mouse," Mr. Martin said. "I seem to have a problem." The neighborhood was quiet and I was on our front porch, reading, so I could hear as he explained how he'd locked himself out of his garage, and how there was a small window, tiny, around the back, that he didn't think he'd fit through, but

Mouse surely would, and I remember hearing her agree, and it follows that I must have heard the garage door grind open and then fall shut again, but I don't remember noticing. I remember that she was gone a long time, and that I got impatient, because I'd decided I wanted to play Boat after all, and I wanted to hear what Mr. Martin's garage looked like on the inside, and then I remember being annoyed because when Mouse finally came back to our house she wouldn't play Boat, and she wouldn't tell me about Mr. Martin's garage. She wouldn't tell me anything. She just shrugged and went to her room, and it was a long time before I could make her come out.

It was late afternoon, and we thought people might be sitting down to Sunday dinner, so Leo swung by the Neosho County Animal Impoundment Facility. It's not a real pound, like in an old cartoon, but where the cops put the dogs who've been seized, taken from abusive homes, or the really messed-up strays. Nobody cares what happens to them anymore; the cops aren't like the Humane Society, checking you out to see if you can provide your Time and Love and A Little Piece of Yourself to every adoptee. The cops just want the crazy dogs out of their hair, so they don't ask too many questions. Leo pulled the van right up to the gates, the back outfitted with his cages and kennels, the poodle and the lab and terrier in there already yelping at each other. Should have raised everybody's eyebrows, and instead they're all like, how convenient. You came prepared. Leo picked out two, a boxer mix and a pinscher mix. The cops had already had the dogs' toenails cut down, and Leo was wearing gloves, so he got them muzzled and in the back all right. Once the van started up, though, the new dogs howled and barked and rattled around. "Listen to that racket back there," Leo said. "Good riddance, am I right?"

The summer Mouse locked herself in the fridge I'd find her with popsicles, the kind that pull apart, and I'd ask her for halves, but she'd refuse to share. I spied on her, and found out that she got them from Mr. Martin, as thanks for unlocking his garage door from the inside, which she seemed to have to do a lot those days, and I wondered if Mr. Martin was much older than he looked, and was getting to be the forgetful kind of crazy that old people got to be. I asked her if the next time Mr. Martin locked himself out I could open the door for him, and get a popsicle, and when she looked at me and shook her head, I called her selfish.

We were driving back through Webb City to get on the highway, head home for the day, when I saw the FOUND DOG sign. We were stopped at a red light, and I put my finger on the car window where the sign was, so if you squinted my index finger was petting the Dalmatian's head. "That's a gorgeous dog," I said. "The owner must be freaking out."

Leo looked over where I was pointing, and instead of going straight on green he turned right, pulled over, hopped out and tore the flyer off the pole. "Truman Street," he said. "You know where that is?"

"I can look at the map," I said, and I did, without even asking him why he wanted to know. I didn't think we'd go there; that's how dumb I am, sometimes.

"What do you think?" Leo asked. "Should we give it a shot?"

"Give what a shot?"

He held the flyer up next to his face, like he was asking if I thought there was a resemblance.

"It's not for taking," I said. "They're just looking for the owner."

"They been looking for a while," Leo said, shaking the paper. The flyer was stiff and rumpled, like it had gotten rained on and had time to dry.

"It rained yesterday. We don't know how long that's been up."

"Let me just find out then. Let me call and see if they've still got the dog."

I didn't see the harm in that, maybe because I don't see a lot of things I ought to. The dog hadn't been picked up, and when Leo made a sound in his throat like joy, like relief, when he thanked the person on the phone for making up those flyers, I knew we were locked into going.

"You don't even know the dog's name," I said on the way

over, trying to protest and navigate at the same time, which didn't work out so well because the whole time I was giving reasons not to go, I was interrupting myself with the turns he had to make to get there.

"I can do this," he said.

"The dog belongs to someone. It probably ran away and some poor family is tearing their hair out looking for it."

"Since when do you care about that?"

"Since always. You bunch unwanted dogs. This is a Wanted Dog."

"I want it."

"It's Wanted by someone who isn't just going to sell it on in a week for a little cash."

"Not a little. A lot of cash. Jorgen told me at the market in Lamar that Parke-Davis needs Dalmatians. They want to test an eye medication. Something to do with all the genetic blindness in the breed. They're paying top dollar."

"To Jorgen. Not to you."

"He'll give a fair cut."

I studied the picture on the flyer. "I don't think this one's blind."

"Doesn't need to be. They want sighted ones, too. Controls, or maybe they drug them and then blind them or something."

"You're a jerk," I said, but Leo didn't think I meant it.

When I found Mouse in the fridge, I called her stupid. "Stupid stupid stupid," I said. "You stuck yourself in a refrigerator." I pronounced all five syllables of the word, because maybe I didn't get to open garage doors and eat double-sized popsicles, but I was her big sister, and Mouse had better learn it.

"I'm *hiding*," Mouse said, and I noticed that she'd been crying but didn't seem scared, not of running out of air or being trapped forever with her feet in a crisper drawer.

"Fine," I said, because I'd expected her to be grateful to me for finding her and letting her out, and instead I was learning that she wasn't scared of any of the things I'd be scared of, and I didn't understand anymore what did scare her. "Hide, then." I shut the door on her, and when I finally opened it she tried to bolt past me, like the raccoons when we startled them, but she was all folded up from being squeezed in the fridge, and she fell out on her knees. I laughed at her as she picked herself up and walked across the yard into our house. She felt very far away then, and I followed to catch up, but even when we were in the same room after that the feeling stayed, like I'd stretched one of her hair ties too far and made it useless as a string, all the elastic gone out of it.

Leo went up the front walk of 1206 Truman Street with a leash slung over his shoulder, a pink nylon collar dangling down his back. The flyer had said "she," so Leo took the collar off Muffy, the dead woman's poodle, and attached a lead. He left Muffy's tags in the driver's side drink holder.

He rang the doorbell, which set a dog to barking somewhere inside. The man who answered the door was bald on top, round about the middle, with a polo shirt and a nice smile. Leo was still shaking his hand, saying "Hello, Mr. Minton. Dale, if that's all right," when the Dalmatian came up behind the man and pressed its head between his legs, barking at Leo. Not aggressive, but curious, just checking out what's what. Leo knelt down and caught the dog's collar, leaning over her so all Dale Minton could see was the top of Leo's head, his shiny hair, pulled back neat. I could see Leo reaching for the collar, catching the tags between his fingers for a quick glance. "Perdita," he said. "Oh, Honey. I've been worried sick."

"Perdita. Like the Disney movie," I said. "*101 Dalmations.*"

Leo glared, because I wasn't helping.

"Yeah," Dale said. "My kids loved the name. They have the movie on video."

"Is that right?" Leo said, admiringly.

"So this is your dog, then?"

"Sure is. Where'd you find her?"

"Out in the street. We worried she'd get hit."

"My wife thinks she left the gate open, and Perdita's got a wandering streak." Leo let his hands roam over Perdita's head, behind her flapping ears, under them, down her neck and under her muzzle. He reached for her belly and stroked her sides. He found a place on her stomach that made her sigh, and pulled back to let Dale see. "She always seems to have an itch right about here," Leo said, and drove his fingers in until the dog whuffed and turned her head up to lick Leo's face. "Bit tricky to find, but scratch it and she's yours forever."

"Is there a Pongo?"

"Like the movie? We'd like to, someday. A Pongo and some puppies, Rolly and Dopey and Dancer and Vixen, or whatever they were."

"Dopey's a dwarf," I said. "And the other two were reindeer."

"Then I'll let you do the naming, Honey," Leo said, and the voice he used with me was a lot sharper than the one he used with the dog.

After that things went fast. Leo was gearing up for more questions, where we lived, how long we'd had the dog, but Dale seemed satisfied. Perdita was in heaven, and Leo looked in love, bending his face down so her long, flat, tongue could lick his cheek. Dale called the kids into the front hall to say their goodbyes, and Leo offered him some reward money. Dale shook his head. He seemed like an upstanding kind of guy. When we pulled away I had Perdita in my lap. I assumed Leo would pull over in a couple of streets to move her to the back, but he never did. We drove the forty-five minutes home that way, with the dog cradled in my lap, her head out the window, tongue hanging out, drooling for joy.

At home Leo got the dogs settled in the kennels out back. It was a good haul, he said, all hale and healthy, serum dogs for sure. That's not saying all that much. A dog only needs to look like it'll last seven days to be a serum dog. After that it's a question of degree. Acute dogs look likely to drop dead in twenty-four hours or less. The laboratories don't have much use for them. They're sold lot rate, in bulk, like coffee beans at the supermarket. Leo doesn't have the USDA license to sell direct, but Jorgen does. There are lots of regulars, all Class B Dealer licensed. They show up at the Pick-n-Trades, the flea markets, all over Neosho County. After the dogs are out of Leo's hands, they're on their way to a lab. Pharmaceuticals, or cosmetics, biology departments or medical schools. Leo bunches regular and knows what he's doing: good breeds, good animals, healthy enough to bring serum price. He'll come home with as much in his pocket as a week at National Beef.

The first night Perdita was caged out back she howled for hours. The moon was almost full, soft and yellow like an egg yolk. I tried to sleep, pressed my head down into the pillow, into the curve of Leo's shoulder, which is bony but still nice to sleep on. I tried to wedge my hands against my ears, but I couldn't not-hear the way I'm used to. I got out of bed and went outside. Some of the dogs were sleeping, the old hands, the slow breathing inmates who didn't pay Perdita any mind. The dogs from today, the poodle, the terrier, the chocolate lab, the boxer and the pinscher, were all anxious. Perdita stopped howling for a moment to look at me, then just tilted her head back up and screamed. The moon was bright and her white coat glowed, with the spots standing out like little patches of night, spreading, eating away at her like Leo's gangrene, until there'd be no glowing left. Her teeth were shiny and the light made her eyes look bright and flat. There was a breeze that whipped between my knees and under the long T-shirt I wear to bed, but there was no one to be modest for except the dogs. I stepped closer to the kennels and the grass under my feet went to dirt, packed hard and scrabbled by dog toes. I put my hand on the latch to Perdita's cage. I stood there, just like that, thinking about all the useless things that might happen if I let her go. The way she might be hit by a truck on the highway trying to scent her way cross-county, or how Leo'd be angry but mostly just confused, at why I'd do a thing like that, take money out of his pocket and bread off our table. How Leo'd always been decent to me, but I'd seen the unkindness in him, and I didn't want to see it again pointed in my direction. How if Perdita had managed to get lost in Webb City, she'd probably never find home from way out here. How if I let her out, not much good would come of it for anyone. She'd stopped howling while I stood there, looking at me with eyes that were probably supposed to be pleading, but in the night were flat and fierce and reflective. "Sorry, Honey," I said, and stepped away from the cage, and the dog started up again, piercing and pathetic. She howled every night for the week before Joplin, until Leo came home without her and I slept a little better.

The summer Mouse locked herself in a fridge, and Mr. Martin locked himself out of his own garage, over and over, the only thing I ever noticed was how Mouse had popsicles and wouldn't share. I was angry at her and for a long time that was all I remembered about that summer. I couldn't even tell you when she stopped having popsicles, or when Mr. Martin finally had the rotting furniture hauled away, or when I realized that I had never been able to protect her, not ever, and that whatever's good about her life now is in spite of me just like it's in spite of Mom and Mr. Martin and everybody else, and that if I had the opportunity to steal again for her, I'd steal big. Something better than butter, better than a dog, because I let her go away from me and into a garage again and again, and whatever I'm doing now is nothing compared to that.

Joplin was a month ago, so the rottie's probably dead by now, and the poodle, the terrier, the lab. I assume Perdita's dead, too. It seems dangerous to think otherwise. If she isn't, I should probably be wishing for her that she was, but mostly I've got enough on my plate without worrying about the dogs. Mouse still sends me the same dumb postcards. The Goodwill still pays six an hour. Leo's still elbow deep in cow brains. His skin thing is getting worse. He's got patches so bad they're swampy with fluid, where his shirts stick and scabs won't form. He's always been hourly at National Beef so there's no insurance. It's like he's molting into something new and horrible, and all I want to do is hold his skin closed, press the seams of him together, so he won't fall apart and nothing in our lives will change, because I figure I'm about as happy as I'm going to get the way things are. So I refuse to wish Leo nice, or the dogs free, or my sister happy, or myself forgiven, or much of anything all that much different than it's likely to get. I just won't wish them, and then when they all don't happen it won't mean a thing to me. If this is what I get in this world I'll take it. Love and squalor, but mostly love. I'll take it and I'll take it and I will not be sorry.

Embodied

In this, my 127th life, I am employed as an internal auditor with Wells Fargo. I live in Des Moines, Iowa, in a white, three-bedroom house. I have a husband named Murray, and six months ago I had a baby son named Jacob. I don't have him anymore.

Murray's good with kids. He teaches the fourth grade. He's the only man on staff at Haisley Elementary apart from the gym teacher and the janitor, so he gets fussed over. I can't tell if he likes it or if he's lonely. I went to the Haisley Curriculum Night with Murray this past spring, just to be supportive, look at the projects his students had been working on. They were the same ones he does every year, the self-portraits in pastels, the informational posters on native bird species, the puppets of Harriet Tubman, Matthew Henson, Martin Luther King, Jr. for Black History Month. I sat up front at Murray's desk while he talked to the parents, telling them about the curricular goals for the fourth-grade year and the upcoming Iowa Standardized Educational Assessment Tests. I'd started showing and it made people tender with me. They offered me seats, brought me fruit punch in paper cups.

"Mr. Rankin's so good with the children," they said. "He must be so excited."

The parents were polite to me, but distant, too, like I was breeding something on Murray's behalf. Still, it's always nice to see someone you care for be complimented, recognized, given plates of cookies and African violets in orange plastic pots. At home our windowsills are filled with African violets, tiny purple flowers and thick fuzzy green leaves. I kill them deliberately. If I didn't, the whole house would fill up with them.

"Is it your first?" the parents asked, and I nodded.

In fact, over 127 lives I've been pregnant something like 200, maybe 220 times. The numbers get a little hazy. But I figured I knew what to expect. We'd decided to try for a baby, and I'd gotten pregnant quickly. The first few weeks, we were both excited. But when I was sick in the mornings, when my belly seized around itself, I could feel that something was wrong.

There were a few kids at Curriculum Night, even though they weren't supposed to be there. Their parents said they couldn't find babysitters. The kids were bouncing off the walls, full of fruit punch and sugar cookies, and Murray finally made them go stand out in the hall. He didn't let them back in until their parents were ready to leave. When he opened the door the kids shot back in, unrepentant, and knocked over three of the child-sized blue plastic chairs and a desk. "You're sure you want one?" I asked, hand on my belly. It was early enough that I was still hoping that one of those days he might just say "no," and we could call the whole thing off.

"Ours will be different," he said, locking his classroom door behind us. We headed out to the parking lot. We lived a few blocks from the school, but it was early spring and the weather was uncertain, so we'd taken my car.

"Isn't that what all teachers say? 'Mine will be different?'"

"Mine *will* be different."

"You say that now."

"I'm sure *I'll* be different. Every kid in my class, I've wanted to pitch 'em out the window some day or other. You have to remind yourself that you just can't do it, you tell yourself to care about them. I'm looking forward to having a kid that I don't have to remind myself not to want to do some damage to."

"And if we end up with a hellion?"

"We'll love it anyway. We won't have a choice. We'll be parents: automatic affection."

Murray was right about one thing: we don't have a choice. The heart hates who it hates.

I don't have a lot of experience with hatred, really. Resignation, perhaps. Reincarnation is definitely a lesson in socio-economics. I've been aristocracy exactly twice. The rest of the time I've been here shoveling shit with everyone else. This current life is, objectively, the best of my existence. It's not that I'm comparing the life of a Certified Internal Auditor with stimulating evenings conversing in Mme. de Staël's celebrated salon in the Marais. I'm comparing it to dying in childbirth, working someone else's land, getting smallpox and typhoid and cholera and malaria and dengue fever. A good office job isn't something you just throw away.

As a side note, one of my turns among the royals was in 1296, when I was one of nine princes of Georgia, exactly 505 years before the country was annexed by Russia. All nine of us were named David Melnik, David the King. It got confusing. Coincidentally, Melnik is also the name of a town in northern Bohemia, where in a different life my family made wine. We had beautiful vineyards and a decent life, and my parents were very upset when I went off to fight with the Hussites. I wasn't aware of this life until recently, when Lorna, from work, went there on vacation and showed her photos around the breakroom during lunch. She'd been to a church decorated entirely in bones: a bone chandelier, a bone altar, bone candelabras, and a display of skulls smashed and shot through during the Hussite wars. One of them was mine, the second from the left, on the bottom shelf. It looked dusty. I don't know what it was that felt familiar; even I've never seen my own skull. I kept staring at the photograph, holding up the rotation, photos stacking up to my right and Nick and Garrison, to my left, twiddling their thumbs over a photo of Lorna's ugly fiancé in his boxers on a hotel balcony.

"Are you okay?" Lorna asked.

"I'm fine," I said, and I passed the picture on to Nick. I let go of the only evidence I'll ever have that that yellowed, brittle hump of bone used to be me, that when the musket ball killed me with an explosive, sudden pressure, I was a young man named Vojta who would never own a vineyard, who would never sleep with a woman, who would not receive the reward he expected from the God he fought for.

I certainly didn't say anything there in the breakroom, not to Lorna and definitely not to Nick or Garrison. I know how it sounds. Give me credit for a sense of self-preservation. I'm an audit project leader in the central Midwestern regional office of the largest financial institution headquartered in the western U.S. I have plans at Wells Fargo. I'm aiming for a transfer to corporate headquarters in San Francisco within the next five years. This isn't hoodoo spirituality; it's just fact, squared up and solid like my Q4 internal audit of the personal banking division. We're all trailing these lives out behind us, dragging them along like a dress train or a tail or a jet plume. I'm just one of the only ones who sees them.

As lives go, this one's okay. Des Moines isn't fin-de-siècle Paris, or Old Kingdom Cairo, but there's enough to do and growing up in Sioux Falls would make about anywhere look like someplace worth spending a few decades. Anyway, it's not really as confusing as you'd think, being the 127th version of yourself. I remember my other lives the way I remember that I need to buy milk on the way home from work, or that I need to pay the water bill, or call my father on his birthday. They're quiet, in the background, a little hush of white noise, like the sea in a shell. In this life, I've seen the sea only once, on a family vacation to Florida. I think people from dry places lack a certain respect for the ocean. I've known the sea as a killing thing. I've been a fisherman, several times. Once a whaler, once a clamdigger and once a life in which I dove for abalone. When I died I left a widow and three children, the third of whom I did not love. I don't know what it was about him, my son who dove for abalone with me and slept across the room in our house by the sea, but I did not love him, and it shamed me that he knew.

"Murray," I said, a couple of weeks after Curriculum Night. He was lying on the couch, watching the History Channel. He watches a lot of educational shows looking for things he can screen in his classroom, kill forty-five minutes. We have piles of blank tapes at the ready on top of the television. I walked in front of him, sat on the coffee table. "It doesn't feel right," I said. "It feels strange." I held my hands over my belly, the swell of it, still small and low between my hip bones.

"What do you mean?"

"I just have a bad feeling," I said. It sounded stupid, like I'd seen *Rosemary's Baby* once too often, but I couldn't think of any other way to explain it. I've spoken 109 different languages, and I hunted through all the bits and pieces I could remember of them. But it was like when I go back in my mind as far as I can: there's a cave, and a lot of grunting, and I had thoughts I couldn't think because I didn't have the words. I didn't have the tongue, the larynx that I needed to pronounce words in Tagalog, or Swahili, or Old Provençal, which was quite new at the time I spoke it, or English. I give English a six on an overall scale of difficulty. It is a much easier language to master than we like to think.

Murray opened his mouth and shut it a few times, and I could tell that he was searching through the one language he'd ever learned to find the right thing to say. "When's your next appointment with Dr. Lyons?" he asked.

"In a week."

"You should tell her. You should ask her about it." Murray was frightened but it backfired on me; he wanted so badly to believe that nothing was wrong that it made him dismissive. I wanted his pity and his panic and I wanted rescue. He wanted to wait it out until the next scheduled appointment, until the ultrasound. He said I could call my Ob/Gyn if I really wanted. But what would I tell her? That I had been pregnant hundreds of times and this was different from any of them? That I was choking on my own baby?

If I could have told anyone, it would have been Murray. He knows about my other lives, that I remember things no one else does and that perhaps no one should. They make me tired, when I think about them too long. Bone-tired like when you feel too exhausted to sleep, only when I feel that way it's worse because I don't know if I'll ever get to sleep, if we ever get to stop, or if we just go on forever. I don't believe in nirvana. I don't think we ever get it right. I don't feel any wiser than I did in that cave. It scares me, what that might mean, that there might not be any stop to it, no punishment or paradise or just oblivion.

Murray doesn't mind that I don't go to church with him. I think he gets extra attention from the ladies: how sad, that your wife sleeps in on Sundays, that it takes her a cup of coffee and two sections of the paper (front page and Arts and Leisure) to be civil. Murray's an Episcopalian anyway, and if I did decide to start going to church again, it wouldn't be to St. Andrew's. They're just Catholics with no pope, and I haven't died for five separate faiths just to turn around and attend a church that only exists because some English king wanted to trade up on wives. In this life I was raised a Methodist. I didn't mind it at the time. As a kid I was just living the one life, only aware of having eight years under my belt, not 5,000-odd. If you're counting, that works out to an average life expectancy, over 127 lives, of about forty. When I think that I'm only ten years short of that right now, it helps put things in perspective.

The routine ultrasound was scheduled for eighteen weeks. The baby quickened at seventeen and I flinched every time I felt it move, just a flutter, like prickles on the back of your neck except that it was inside me and it was hateful to me and there was no way to make it stop. I held a thing inside of myself that felt heavy and corrosive, that I wanted desperately to be rid of. How to say that I was hoping for a monster? For something limbless, hopeless, so damaged no one would ask me to carry it to term. It would have been a relief to find out that my dread was prescient, that it had a source and a solution. But he was fine, two arms, two legs, ten fingers, ten toes, one head with one mouth and one nose and two eyes, still fused shut. He turned out to be a he, everything where it should be. Murray was ecstatic, so relieved I almost thought he'd keel over right there in the examining room and I wanted to go to him, but I was flat on my back, my belly covered in goo and my baby pulsing there on the screen in black and white.

He insisted we go out to dinner, to celebrate. He ordered wine for himself and then looked at me guiltily. "Go ahead," I said. "You deserve it. I've been making you so nervous, all over nothing."

"Not nothing," he said. "I know you've been feeling rotten. It's not that I don't think you have. It's just such a relief. That the baby's healthy."

"I know. I feel the same way," I said, which is possibly the second biggest lie I've ever told him.

Murray liked the name Jacob, and I didn't dislike it. "Are you sure?" he asked. "You don't seem thrilled."

"Jacob's fine," I said. The service was slow, and I felt ill and ravenous at the same time. I ate most of the bread and got crumbs all over the tablecloth. I resented being so hungry, resented that the bread I ate was being used to grow something that sapped me like a parasite.

"It doesn't have to be Jacob. Did you know an obnoxious Jacob? Like I couldn't ever name my son Paul, there was this horrible kid when I was in fifth grade, he was such a bully. I'd understand."

There seemed to be nothing Murray was not willing to understand. It made him seem less intelligent, like he wasn't so much making allowances for people as just not noticing what made them difficult in the first place. It's an unfair thing, kindness making people out to be dumber than they are.

"Jacob's fine."

"Are you thinking of Jacobs from—before? From other lives?" He's the only one who can say things like that and make them sound natural, who can even say them with a straight face. I've never known if he's just humoring me or not, if he really believes me or just finds my other qualities compelling enough to make up for being delusional. I feel like it should bother me more than it does, not knowing if my husband secretly thinks I'm crazy. Maybe I don't mind because I have secrets about him, too, such as the fact that the way in which I love him is almost the exact same way in which I loved my wife in China, in 1102. I'd passed the exams to enter government service, and I had to go see a district official, in the provincial capital, to be assigned to a post. I didn't know where the rest of my life would take place and it frightened me. But my parents were very proud, and they helped to arrange a marriage with a girl who was solemn but pretty. We had five children, and they looked just like somebody had taken half of me and half of her and mixed them until they balanced exactly. We enjoyed each other's company and did not expect more than life was likely to provide. Our happiness might have been a matter of managed expectations, but it was real.

I've never told Murray because I don't want to hurt him, to imply that my love for him is recycled. Because I think maybe he really does believe me, and I don't want to repay his trust with reconstituted love. Besides, I'm not sure he'd understand the distinction, that I don't think he *is* my wife, reincarnated, just that he reminds me of her. There's a big difference. I don't know who he used to be; he's a soul I've never encountered, and while it makes him an unknown quantity, it's a thing to be grateful for. It's horrible to see someone and recognize who they were before and then be unable to see who they are now, to react to them in a way that's out of my control, that has nothing to do with this life. It's only happened once or twice, but that was enough. I had to quit my work-study job in college because my boss turned out to be someone I'd killed. The details were fuzzy, but the guilt was sharp and overwhelming. I couldn't see the Dining Services Supervisor who signed off on my time cards: just the soldier, the look of pain and disbelief.

"Jacob's fine with me," I told Murray, that night at the restaurant, after the ultrasound. "It's fine."

Murray buttered the last piece of bread and put it on the plate in front of me. "You should pick the middle name," he said.

"I'll think of something," I said. "Jacob-something-Rankin. It'll be a good name."

I've known a lot of Jacobs. Yacoub worked in the tanneries in Fez and wore a pair of bright yellow shoes he'd dyed himself. It was ugly work, and he was considered unclean for doing it. The fumes from the dyes were burning away his lungs, but we didn't know. Our sons went to the tanneries when they were grown, and I'm glad none of us understood that it would kill them, too. The name wasn't the problem. If I flinched at every name I've known before, I'd never be able to look at anyone straightways. But his having a name at all made the feeling worse. Jacob got bigger and would kick me, hard and constant and spiteful, and Murray would say, "Feel that," like I had a choice. "Feel what a powerful little kid that's going to be."

One evening when Murray was out, Jacob was thrashing like mad. I tried to distract myself, to read a book or watch TV. I wanted Murray to come home, but I knew it wouldn't be 'til late. The second Saturday of every month he went over to a friend's house to play poker. Murray grew up around here, and his friends are still friends from high school. They're good guys, but they treat him badly sometimes, maybe because he's the one who went to college, who works in a school, who does a job women do and has a wife who makes more than he does and who lives in the nicest house of any of them because of it. They gang up on him, make sure he leaves the table with less money than he started with, no matter which of them ends up with it. They think he doesn't know, but he does, and plays with them anyway.

Jacob kept on kicking me, and finally I hit him back, lifted up my shirt and slapped my belly, hard, several times. I shouted at the baby to stop, I told him that I hated him, and eventually he went still. I managed to bruise myself, a violet smudge above my left hip. It was stupid. Murray saw it and asked what had happened. I told him I hadn't noticed anything, and he scolded me to be careful.

"I wonder if he'll remember being other people," Murray said one morning, slow and sleepy. It was Saturday and we were still in bed. I'd always slept on my back before, and I didn't sleep so well now that I had to lie on my side. It was one of the moments that made me think he believed me, that he took on faith everything I'd ever said about myself. I didn't think he had it in him to bait me, to try to draw me out like that if he didn't.

"I didn't remember right away," I said. It had taken me until the spring of my third-grade year. The big fads that year were slap bracelets and demon possession. The bracelets were flat strips of neon plastic that coiled around your wrist when you slapped them to your skin. The demon possession fad started when Amber Novotny, the most popular girl in the third grade, had a grand mal seizure during art class. She fell off her stool, knocking her watercolors to the floor. Yogurt cups filled with dirty water spilled and pooled around her head as she thrashed and then lay still. It was one of the most amazing things I'd ever seen.

Later that day during recess, one of Amber's best friends, maybe worried that Amber's epilepsy would be considered distinctly un-cool, told us a thrilling tale of the demon that was struggling for Amber's soul, trying to take up residence in her skin, to unwrap all her birthday presents and take the lead in the class play. Amber had been fighting bravely, battling the demon in unsung silence. It was marvelous and horrifying. We all wanted one, a demon of our own, to name and invent long tales of struggle against. During recess we would stand in circles and recount these tales to each other, and when the playground supervisors' backs were turned, drop twitching into the grass.

When it came time to name my own demon, describe its fiendish designs on my immortal soul, my answer came easily, swift and unexpected. I asked myself who else might be living in my skin and there she was, the first one I remembered. She was named Sally, I told the other children, and they groaned. Sally was no name for a demon, but she wasn't one. She was an English woman, born in 1795. A thief and, although I didn't realize it at the time, a prostitute. I had no idea what to make of her memories of a succession of men, the way they held her and pushed inside her. She was transported to Sydney in 1819.

I wonder if I have descendants in Australia, and if I do, if they live somewhere scenic. I have fantasies of taking a round-the-world trip someday, staying for free in the homes of all the people I'm related to, all the people who would not be alive on earth at this present moment without me. But there's no way to ask them. I lose track of all the people I loved or hated, or just knew, indifferently. I don't know what happens to them, what kind of lives they go on to lead. I couldn't tell that morning if Murray wanted Jacob to remember, if he thought I had some special gene, and was hoping that it was dominant instead of recessive. I think he's jealous of me sometimes, that I've experienced so much. He doesn't listen when I try to explain that all he's missing out on is heartache.

Jacob Alan Rankin was born by scheduled cesarean in the 42nd week. I'd picked Alan because I disliked it, purely a matter of aesthetics, not of bad associations. I'd grown so angry with the child I didn't want to give him a name I cared for. I had to have a cesarean because the birth presentation was a breech, not feet first, but knees first, kneeling, Jacob's arms in front of his chest and his hands pressed together like he was praying. He was born perfect: no claws, no fangs, no horns. Since he hadn't had to squeeze through the birth canal, his head was still flawlessly round; he stood out in the nursery from all the red-faced cone-head babies. A woman from La Leche League gave me a lesson on breast-feeding, which I didn't need. Inuit women used to breast-feed their children up to the age of five. It creates a powerful mother-child bond. Perhaps too powerful. My second son never looked for a wife, but seemed content to stay by me. I appreciated his help, but it made me wonder if I'd done something wrong that had stunted him, shrunk his life and tied him too closely to me. Jacob not nursing was not a lack of proper technique. Perhaps he could taste the bitterness in me, how I was recognizing who he was, putting a name and a face to the hate I had when he was inside me. I'd looked at him now. I'd seen who he used to be.

I feel I need to be clear on something: that I don't run around swearing vengeance. Revenge is about satisfaction, but it's also about restoring balance, and I think that's something that enough living wears away, the idea that there's any balance to be restored. I have never expected justice, in any of my 126 other lives, and I've been right not to. I've been done wrong, plenty of times, and done plenty of wrong myself. If I could point to one and say, that was it, that was the Worst Thing, that was the one thing I couldn't forgive, this would all make a lot more sense. But I can't, so let's pause for a minute to lay aside all the microbes, the bacteria and the viruses. We'll lay aside the cancer and the autoimmune diseases and the genetic defects, all the worst surprises the body springs on itself. We'll lay aside a lack of food or water or shelter or warmth. We'll lay aside old age. There's no way to make them answer. We'll lay aside any nonsentient killers, animals who snapped or mauled or gored me out of life. They aren't culpable. Let's lay aside the deaths in battle, the anonymous soldiers who did me in. The anonymous babies that I died trying to birth. None of it was personal.

Something that was personal: that I was drowned once, as a child. I can't remember when, or where, or even why I remember. I don't remember infancy, usually. But I remember being held under the water by my mother, put down like an animal. I don't know who she was or why she did it. But I always knew that if she came back, if I recognized her, I wouldn't be able to forgive her.

The body fights. That's what I remember most from a life I spent in serfdom, working a scythe through wheat. The wheat was high above our heads, and we moved carefully, in a pattern, cutting in the same rhythm, a few paces apart. I got turned around somehow in the field, and when I swung the blade to my right I hit my neighbor's thigh, the femoral artery, and by the time I pressed my hands against the cut his pants were already wet with blood. I remember the way the blood came in the same rhythm as his pulse, his heart beating his own life out. His lungs seized for air. He would not go. I knew I'd killed him, and I wished he'd hurry, that his body would not fight so hard. But the body is an animal thing and does not know how to surrender.

An infant's body fights quietly. Jacob's life was so new, perhaps he didn't know he had anything to lose. In a way he didn't, because there I was, and there he was, the old soul, the hands that held me under. Everything that mattered about me had survived him, and he would survive me. He would become someone else's child, and this abbreviated life, this little mistake, would be behind him. I hoped he would come back in the developed world somewhere, where he could go to school and eat well. I'm not petty. I didn't wish miseries on him. I figured this would make us even.

In the crib: a blue blanket, a large stuffed bear, a cow that said moo when you squeezed it. I thought about the bear, then took one of the pillows from the master bedroom, from my side of the bed, not Murray's. I wouldn't do that to him. It is possible that Jacob never woke. Some infants suffocate themselves against their own mattresses; the brain is so undeveloped it will starve without rousing the body. Perhaps he did wake, and wondered why the world no longer provided the things he needed, the air his lungs clutched for. In any case he didn't move. He didn't flail. There were no muffled cries. The minutes were still and silent and there was no indication that his brain was starving, his heart shivering and erratic and finally failing. When it was over I put the pillow back on my bed. I brushed my teeth, put on my nightgown, and went to sleep.

Murray was at his poker game. I knew when he came home he'd look in on Jacob, not so much to check up on him as just to admire him, feel his own heart lift, feel the rush you get from looking at a child you love helplessly. Murray would be the one to find him. I couldn't think how else to do it, even though the cruelty of it seemed enormous, even to me. He woke me up shouting my name, then Jacob's, then mine again. I called 911 while Murray pressed Jacob's chest with two fingers, breathed into his mouth. When I got off the phone I put a hand on Jacob's arm. It was cool to the touch, and I tried to make Murray stop, but he wouldn't listen to me. The paramedics came and took Jacob out to the ambulance in the driveway. They closed the doors behind them and didn't come out for several minutes. For show, I think, or just getting themselves ready to break the news. Then we all had to wait for the medical examiner to come, the police and the police photographers. I put on a pot of coffee.

I fielded the questions, about how I'd put Jacob to sleep on his back, not his stomach. How I hadn't noticed anything wrong with him. They took photographs of the bedroom, the crib, how the mattress was the right size and softness, how there weren't too many blankets, or pillows, or soft animals, how there wasn't anything anybody could point to that we'd done wrong. The medical examiner took Jacob's body away for an autopsy. The

office telephoned a few hours later, to say they could release
the body, to ask us where we wanted it sent. I picked a funeral
home out of the yellow pages. It was morning by that time, but
Murray was still sitting on the couch, a mug of cold coffee on the
table in front of him. He'd barely moved.

Other relevant facts: that it is impossible to distinguish at
autopsy between Sudden Infant Death Syndrome and accidental
or deliberate suffocation with a soft object. That the possibility
of such suffocation should only be investigated if the parents
have had previous infants die under the same circumstances,
or if both of a set of twins has died. That in all other cases, the
parents should be treated with every courtesy and consideration
for the suddenness of their loss, the depth of their grief, and
the near-assuredness of their innocence. That this was another
webpage I'd minimized at work when the Director of Internal
Auditing came in to talk to me about my upcoming maternity
leave. That the small, soft body I grew inside myself turned out
to be infected with a soul I could not keep. That I couldn't do
it, and that I know there are no words in any of 109 different
languages to defend myself.

Murray's grief has flayed me. He clings to the fact that it's a
sorrow we can share, that we're united in this terrible sadness. It
makes me feel guilty, yes, but also ashamed for him, because he
has no idea how alone he is, the weight of the grief he bears by
himself. I'm light with relief, and I don't know how to be with
him anymore. I'm split to the bone, and when he touches me his
hands are like salt. It's all I can do to lie beside him when we
sleep. Murray says he's ready for another baby, and I'm stiff with
shame. We're both back at work now. We've been out to the
movies, to dinner. Murray went to a basketball game with some
friends last week, although he still won't go play poker. Soon I
won't know what to tell him. I can't tell him that I've hurt him in
a novel, freakish way, a way I never hurt anybody in 5,000 years,
and that I'm finding it hard to match the wrong I've done him to
the practiced love I had for him before, that I still have for him.

I can't tell him that I'd hoped, assumed, that Jacob was an
isolated incident, but that the world's getting crowded. I'm

remembering too much. The new weatherman on the Channel 4 news, or the boy who works Sunday afternoons at the deli counter at Safeway, who's slow with the meat slicer, like he's got all day: I've realized I remember them. I'm recognizing more and more. They're familiar to me and sometimes I miss them and sometimes I hate them and it scares me. I want to tell them that we baked bricks side by side for twenty years, indentured, and invented secrets to tell each other to make the work go faster. That I do not forgive them for taking two more wives after me. That I loved the way they sang or that I was impressed with how well they could track an animal. I can't tell Murray that I haven't recognized him yet, that I look at him and still just see Murray, but that I'm terrified that one day that won't be true.

It's hard for me to keep my mind on things at work. To be an internal auditor, you have to sign a contract promising that you'll demonstrate "professional skepticism." I'm trying, I am. But it's like when I'm going over some shaky accounts, and behind the one set of numbers I can see what's going unsaid. I can see the different breakdowns, different scenarios, different versions of events, what's being hidden by the straight-faced statistics. It's an awful thing, to live in a world that's contracting, backing up on itself like a highway pile-up. It's not a place I understand. I wonder if it would help to get out of Des Moines. If I should concentrate on my career for a while, start applying for corporate transfers. We'd probably have to put off another baby. It's something to run by Murray.

One thing: my dreams have stayed peaceful. They're of daily things. No deaths, no births, no reincarnation. I'm wandering up and down the aisles of the grocery store with no list. I show up at work and I've got an algebra exam. I'm on stage and I've forgotten my lines. Classics. The old naked-in-front-of-a-crowd thing. As far as I know, that's never actually happened to anybody, at least not any of the 127 anybodies I've been. It's something. It's a comfort.

At the Zoo

At the Orangutan Dome the grandfather purchases a plastic cup in the shape of an orangutan head. He offers his grandson a sip. Then he slips behind a tree with the cup and afterwards the boy isn't allowed to drink from it. The boy begs for his own.

Eight dollars for soda in a plastic head, his mother thinks. The flesh-and-blood orangutan is dignified and bored. It sighs and its body deflates. The family turns away toward a glass case labeled *Fennec Fox*. "Look," the grandfather says. "Weasels."

The foxes are tiny, chihuahuas with gold fur and satellite dish ears. "Elephant Weasels can hear things happening in space," the grandfather tells the boy. "They can hear when your tummy rumbles, and they think how much they'd like a little boy to snack on." The boy clutches his grandfather's hand. He believes nearly everything anyone tells him. He has large, serious eyes and a constant look of apprehension that make it easy for his mother to forget his growing size, the way he is too old now for the collapsible stroller she has brought in case he becomes tired. His legs dangle whenever she straps him in with the juice boxes and snacks.

"You know what their favorite foods are?" the grandfather asks. Everyone standing at the enclosure knows—the label lists them—plants, small rodents, lizards and insects. "Elephant weasels love roast beef," the grandfather says. "And key lime pie. And kid stew." He picks up the boy to give him a better view. The people at the enclosure decide they do not care enough to bother saying anything. Let the foxes be weasels. What does it hurt?

The mother does not share their indifference. She grinds her teeth when her father speaks. Her whole life he has been telling these stories, and there was once a time she believed him. As a child she gave Show and Tell presentations on birds that turned out not to exist, on fictive countries whose names were sexual innuendoes she was too young to understand. She was marked down, taken aside by concerned teachers. She still winces at those old humiliations, her own credulity. She has promised herself that her son will grow up on firmer footing.

The grandfather has one hand around the boy and the other around his drink. He gestures with the cup and the orangutan head smacks the glass. The foxes prick their ears toward the sound. Someday, the mother thinks, her father will break her son's gullible little heart.

"Let's see something bigger," he says. "This zoo got any rhinos?"

The mother is a patent lawyer. Her father is in town for the week visiting, and she is using a vacation day rather than leave him alone with her son. She is supposed to be preparing an infringement suit related to proprietary athletic surfacing, patented types of artificial turf and running track. Her husband is a dermatologist, and they will always have enough money, the lawyer and the doctor. On the way to the rhinos the family passes the capybara habitat. "What do *they* eat?" the boy asks.

"Fritos," the grandfather says. "But these might do." He flings a handful of chips over the fence, a new kind of Doritos that were for sale in the Orangutan Dome, Mystery-flavored and slightly green. The chips land in the moat and the capybaras turn their heads to watch. The boy doesn't think that "Mystery" could be anything's favorite flavor. He would like Dum-Dums more, for example, if the "Mystery" suckers did not so often turn out to be root beer. The chips start to dissolve and the capybaras disappear into the reeds. The boy is sad to see them go.

The boy's favorite television shows are all on Animal Planet, and he sobs piteously when anything dies. His favorite stories are all fairy tales. He likes Dora the Explorer and dislikes Bob the Builder. He ties ribbons around the necks of his stuffed animals. It has occurred to his parents that the boy might turn out to be gay and these are the early signs. He is who he is, they tell themselves, whoever that turns out to be. The boy's grandfather finds this repellant.

After the capybaras comes SafariLand. *"Giraffe,"* the son says, when his grandfather points out the neck monsters. His mother wants to cheer.

"Sure, I recognize them now. We rode them, in the war," the grandfather explains. In fact, he has not been in any war. He enlisted after Korea and spent two years in Fort Greely, Alaska. He tells war stories like it's expected of him, like he doesn't know any other way to be an old man, a grandfather. "Giraffes sure can move. Gallop like motherfuckers."

The boy was too excited last night to sleep, and his mother read to him from *The Big Book of Amazing Animal Behavior* to calm him. There is an illustration of an antelope cleaning its nose with its tongue that fascinates and shocks the boy. Sometimes at night he thinks of this picture, the animal with its tongue in its nose. This zoo has several antelope, but none of them are picking their noses. The boy is disappointed. There are oryx, gazelles, Cape hunting dogs, a cheetah. It is midday, and most of the animals are sleeping.

The boy's book explains that elephants are social animals, that the individuals in a family love each other very much. Here at the zoo, he notices that the elephants are caged separately, snorting and kicking at one another. The boy asks his mother why.

A sign explains that the elephants are mentally ill. They are seeing an elephant therapist and taking anti-anxiety medication, but there is some doubt as to whether they will ever be cured. The mother does not want to explain this to her son. She thinks that lawyers are supposed to be better at prevarication, at thinking on their feet, but that has never been the kind of lawyering she was good at. She is good at proprietary athletic surfaces.

It is difficult, however, to stay very interested in athletic surfaces. This is what makes her grateful for the mad scientist who keeps soliciting her counsel in regard to a "temporal transportation device" he invented—he's something different, at least. *I have discovered how to circumvent the problems of the Blinovitch Limitation Effect and the Novikov Self-Consistency Principle,* he wrote in his first letter, sent registered mail. *You're the only one I can trust. This technology has to stay in the right hands.*

The lawyer has no idea why her hands were the right ones, the trusted ones, but there she was, holding the blueprints.

"A time machine," the secretaries said matter-of-factly as they watched her unroll the diagrams on the large table in the conference room. "That's a new one." The secretaries take his packages directly to her office now, lurking until she opens them. The first was a silver gravy boat: *I successfully impersonated a member of King Edward VII's household staff and served him gravy in 1901. Regretfully, I had to abscond with the item to have proof. Thus the price of progress. I hope you do not think me a common criminal.* She has called the other patent law firms in the city, but no one else has been receiving anything stranger than usual. "Someone sent us schematics for wings," another lawyer offered. "The Daedalus 3000. Think it's the same guy?"

In the mother's silence, the grandfather steps in. He can understand what the elephants are saying, he says. He *gets* elephants, like he gets elephant weasels. He comprehends their growls of discomfort and anxiety. "They had a fight this morning," the grandfather says. "Over their toys. They're sulky now, but they'll come around." The only toys the boy sees are tangles of knotted rope, a funnel of food on a post, a pile of hay and some rocks. The boy thinks of his dentist's waiting room with its few *Highlights* magazines and many toothless children. They waggle their loose fangs at the boy, whose own teeth are still small and white and planted firmly in his jaw, then ruin the Hidden Pictures by coloring in what's hidden. The grandfather's explanation makes perfect sense to the boy, and he is curious about what else his grandfather knows. The boy points expectantly at a gazelle.

"Most of the time animals don't say much worthwhile," the grandfather explains. "Anteaters just say 'Ants! Ants! Ants!' And owls say, 'Fly! Hunt! Fly!' And mice say, 'I'm small! I'm frightened! Oh no! An owl! I'm fright—*slurp.*'"

I'm small! I'm frightened! The boy thinks that this is what he feels sometimes, like when other children in daycare take his crayons, when the kids at the dentist threaten to bite. He pictures mice and thinks first, "I'm sorry you're small and frightened; we are the same." Then he thinks, "Not the same. I am much bigger than you. I could hurt you. Perhaps you *should* be frightened." The boy is startled to hear these thoughts inside of him, this excitement at the capacity for harm. "Ants ants ants ants ants ants ants," he whispers on the way to the next enclosure, making a long nose with his arm. He waves the anteater snout in front of him.

"You want to go back to the elephants?" his mother guesses.

The boy is disappointed in her. "Anteater," he explains.

The mad scientist has started writing *For Your Eyes Only* on his envelopes. "Be careful," the secretaries say. "Could be Anthrax." In a padded envelope was a single bullet casing: *I saw this shot fired in 1811 during the expulsion of the Xhosa tribe from the Zuurveld.* He sent a pink skirt, writing, *This may look like a typical flounced Crimplene skirt from the 1960s, but I in fact purchased this item in the year 2206, when mid-twentieth-century fashions enjoy a blessedly brief vogue. 2207 will be all about ponchos.* She has found herself looking, really looking, over the blueprints. The machine isn't familiar: not a DeLorean or Bill and Ted's phonebooth or Doctor Who's police box or any ships she recognizes from *Star Trek* or *Star Wars* or H.G. Wells. It is simply a smooth, metal tube that does not seem, somehow, like something a crazy person would design. She has asked her husband if dermatology holds such surprises. He shrugged. "I didn't know how many mole checks I'd do," he said. "Everyone's worried about skin cancer."

Her father has had a cancer on his cheekbone and one on the top of his left ear. The ear is scarred neatly over but the cheek was recent, and there is still a square white bandage taped across the furrow the doctors dug. They offered to take a skin graft from his thigh to patch it, but he refused. He is proud to not be vain, although he knows that is its own kind of vanity. As a landscaper he took satisfaction in his workingman's tan and powerful shoulders. He retired several years ago, pain in his back, sore knees and elbows. Now the alcohol keeps him loose. He does not like the way his body feels when he is sober. He does not like the way the air touches his cheek when he changes his bandage, the way it brushes something private.

"Hey Kid," the grandfather says. "Do you know why lions eat raw meat?"

The boy shakes his head.

"'Cause they don't know how to cook."

The mother rolls her eyes; her son blinks.

"Why do birds fly south for the winter, Hornswoggle? Too far to walk." When the grandfather isn't calling the boy Tyke or Junior or Hey Kid, he calls him Hornswoggle. No one has any idea why. "What's black and white and red all over? A zebra who didn't know how to cross the road. Which side of a bird has the most feathers? The outside."

The mother is surprised at how many jokes her father knows. How much space are they all taking up? She imagines him shriveling to a pile of wizened bones, a pour of whiskey and a hundred knock-knock jokes. At her mother's wake last year, he told a dirty joke to the women gathered around casseroles in the kitchen. It involved the Pope, Bill Clinton, her dead mother and a donkey. She will not forgive him this.

The most recent package from the mad scientist contained a bolo tie and a potholder, no note. The bolo tie was a mystery. The potholder was a bigger mystery—printed with little cowboy hats and spurs, it looked exactly like one that had hung in her childhood kitchen for years. The potholder makes her long, for the thousandth time that year, to talk to her mother. She wants to laugh together at the impossibility of the mad scientist, to hear her mother say that the potholder had horses instead of spurs, saddles instead of hats, that she has no need for this old anxiousness, the tension between needing to believe and knowing she will be hurt for it, made to look ignorant or gullible. She doesn't know who else she can talk to. Her colleagues would mock her; her son would blink at her; her husband might say something about moles. The mad scientist has been telephoning the firm every day. "Someone's going to have to call him back," the secretaries have said, "someone" meaning her. If she talked to her father, he would—she doesn't know what her father would do. Mix a whiskey and coke in an orangutan head and tell her that if she were less concerned with potholders, she might raise a son who was more of a man.

The grandfather is thinking about dinner. His son-in-law is picking up Chinese carryout, and the grandfather is looking forward to the Kung Pao chicken and Mu Shu pork and the other dishes his grandson will whine about because they smell funny—until the grandfather eats the boy's share. Back at home, the grandfather has been eating poorly. He recently read an item in the paper about someone who stopped leaving the house after his wife of sixty years died. The man ate everything in the fridge, then the freezer, then the cupboard. He ate the last jar of pimentos and then lay down to die. The grandfather has to leave his house to go to the liquor store anyway, so he picks up white bread and peanut butter, corn chips, ice cream. The store is run by a couple whose family still lives in Afghanistan; in the absence of anyone to worry over in an immediate, practical way, they express concern for him. "Vegetables," they say. "You need vegetables, sir."

The mother unfolds the map to look for the anteaters. They are back in The Jungle Experience, near the capybaras. The mother charts a return trip, through The Frozen North and Harsh Deserts: Where Life Fights to Survive. She shows her son the route and asks if he is tired, if he needs to use the stroller. The boy shakes his head.

Already, in spring, the polar bear is wilting. The arctic fox is turning brown. The penguins torpedo acrobatically through glass-walled water. "Look at them playing," the mother says. "Don't they look like they're having fun?" She is holding the boy's hand as she points, so the boy looks up to find his own fist punching the air. "It'd be pretty great to be a penguin, wouldn't it?"

The boy thinks about this. He thinks that this is what people are always saying about children—how great it is to be one. He knows already that an animal's life is not as simple or carefree as it seems. On his favorite program, *Growing Up Walrus*, the zookeepers brought fish for the baby walrus' birthday, but the grown-up walruses stole it and ate it all.

The family walks through the desert. Coyotes pace back and forth. The javelinas wallow amongst heads of lettuce, carrots, and celery. From the side, they are broad, hairy pigs. As the family passes they turn and from the front appear alarmingly narrow, their faces long and their legs close-set. The front of their habitat is decorated with plastic cut-outs of rattlesnakes, cacti, cowboys on horseback.

"Do you remember Mom's old potholder?" the mother asks her father.

"What?"

"The potholder she had for years, with the little hats and spurs on it."

"A potholder? I don't know."

"She said you bought it for her, out west. On your honeymoon."

"Hell, I don't remember. A potholder?"

"Yes, Dad. A potholder."

There is a long silence. "What's black and white and can't get through a revolving door?"

"Never mind."

"A penguin with an arrow through its head."

"I didn't ask."

"Why do you want to know about a potholder?"

The little boy stops them somewhere between desert and jungle, in front of the grizzly bear. The bear is sleeping, but wakes up long enough to defecate, his hind end facing his audience. The bear and the humans watch feces dribble down the wall into the ditch that keeps them separated. Then the bear goes back to sleep, his performance over. The boy watches in awe, whispers, "Gross."

"Nothing," the mother tells her father. "Forget it. I just wanted to know if I was going crazy."

"You're not crazy," the little boy says quietly, down there at the end of her arm.

"Hornswoggle's right," her father says. "I didn't raise crazy."

"You didn't raise anything," the mother says, and regrets it. She is a lawyer and her husband is a doctor and they have an attractive house and a serious, credulous son. Why is it still so important to her to be angry?

The grandfather is dented more than hurt. He is already looking at this moment from a certain remove. The orangutan head is buoyant in his hand. Sun pours through it and makes a splotch of light on the ground.

"I didn't mean that," his daughter says.

"I remember the potholder."

"Really?"

"Maybe. Spurs and hats?"

"What happened to it?"

"Your mother threw it out, far as I remember. It was older than you. Got dirty. It was a potholder. Why?"

The woman looks at her father. What doesn't entertain him he finds uninteresting, easy to dismiss. But he's always found ways to make his daughter amusing. He'd thought she was a funny child, the stories he told and the way she'd believed them. Even the way she got scared of him, sometimes, when a cheerful drunk turned sour, or when she decided she didn't want to play along. He once dropped a banana peel in front of her and when she stepped decorously over it, shoved her to the ground. "Slip, goddamnit," he said, and laughed as her rear end smacked hard against the floor.

"No reason," she says. "I just thought of it. The javelina cage."

"It was a gift," he confirms. "I gave it to your mother." He wants this statement, the old gesture, to carry weight it cannot bear. He wants it to communicate something it does not. Or maybe it says plenty. Who gives his beloved a potholder on their honeymoon? *We laughed about it,* he wants to add, to make sure he is understood. *We thought the western stuff was funny, all the turquoise and headdresses and belt buckles. Your mom bought me a bolo tie. Not to wear, she knew I wouldn't. Just to keep. You wouldn't have ever seen it. It's in a box in my sock drawer and hurts now to look at.* The father looks at his daughter until she looks at the grizzly bear. It is still asleep. She leans toward it, putting her hands on the fence. Her father looks at them, her elegant fingers and the veins beginning to show beneath the skin. He wishes he had not noticed this about his daughter, her veins, not because they make him feel old—he feels old all the time—but because they mean his daughter is aging, that she will end the way her mother did. He will not be there to see it, but his grandson will, barring accident, barring a violation in the normal order of events. He looks away from his daughter's hands and asks, "Where's Hornswoggle?"

The boy has let go of his mother's hand. The boy is missing. His mother whirls in such panic that the grizzly raises its head. The mother is calling and calling and running and the grandfather picks up the things she has left at the fence, the collapsible stroller and the bag of snacks. The man thinks of the boy's soft little legs. How far could he have gotten? Good for you, the man even thinks. Showing a little gumption. He watches his daughter run ahead and then circle back toward the penguins and coyotes. He realizes she is thinking not so much of distance or human predators, but of the animals, of the primeval plight of a human boy in the wild. He tries to picture the unlikely series of events it would take for his grandson to end up drowned in the penguin pool or eaten by coyotes, and he begins to laugh.

The mother runs back from the arctic and the desert and when she sees her father laughing she could kill him. He obviously finds this funny, this crisis that any decent person would respond to with concern. She wants nothing more in that moment than to upend him into the grizzly ditch where the bear can disembowel him.

The man watches his daughter hate him and says, "He's at the anteater." This is all of a sudden a fact, comforting and obvious. The mother is still imagining the orangutan cup sailing into the rocky enclosure along with her father, the bear licking up the drink as a digestif. She runs empty-handed toward the anteater. The old man follows with the bag and stroller.

The boy is too short to see over the fence, so he is crouched at its base, looking at the anteater between the rails. The anteater has a baby that rides on her back as she circles the enclosure. The boy is waggling his arm in front of his face and chanting, "Ants ants ants." There are two human families at the enclosure and both have assumed the boy belongs to the other one. Everyone is startled when his mother rushes up shouting and grabs the boy from behind. The boy, terrified, accidentally hits himself in the face with his own arm. One of the other family's babies starts crying. The anteater stops her circling to secret her child in a wooden shelter. The boy is startled and frightened and his nose stings where he hit it and now the anteater is going away and he is crying. His mother clutches him harder and presses their heads together until the boy's skull hurts. The grandfather arrives, hoping he is forgiven now for laughing, but he can see in his daughter's eyes as she looks at him that he is not. The boy is still sobbing, wriggling now, trying to get down.

"Put him down," the grandfather says. "He wants to get down." His daughter is still rocking the boy. She is usually so calm, so businesslike. It is frustrating to see her undone by a boy watching an anteater. Is this what it would take for her to consider him redeemable, this blind ridiculous panic? "Let him down," the grandfather says, and his daughter ignores him and he thinks he could perhaps make his daughter understand if the boy would just shut up. "Stop fucking crying," the grandfather yells. "Just stop it." Everyone quiets, but the grandfather can't remember now what he'd planned to fill the silence. The straw rattles emptily around the orangutan head as he searches for something to say. "You think the anteater wants to hear that? You think it's got anywhere else it can go? All these animals are stuck here for your benefit, kid. So shut up and get down off your mother and learn something."

As soon as the outburst is over, both mother and grandfather wait for it to shatter the boy completely. But instead he stops crying, because his grandfather has given him something to think about. As his mother lowers him to the ground he looks for the anteater in her small, dusty shelter. The boy thrusts his arms through the fence rails and opens and closes his fists. He thinks about being on the other side of the bars and how the animals never get to go anywhere, not ever. He thinks of all his favorite television shows, the walruses of *Growing Up Walrus* and the meerkats of *Meerkat Manor* and the crocodiles of *The Crocodile Hunter*. Are those animals trapped, too? He'd begged for the zoo, and the zoo is a terrible place.

The boy begins to cry again. The mother hugs him, tries to get him to drink some juice, but he can't stop. His chest heaves and snot runs from his nose. She sighs and opens the collapsible stroller and straps him in and says, "It's time to go home, Honey." People turn to watch them pass, the old man and the woman and the sobbing boy, whose body is too large for the stroller. Other parents shake their heads and think that if he were their child, he would be better behaved. A school group is waiting for a bus outside. One of their chaperones audibly clucks her tongue as the family passes. "Fuck you," the grandfather tells her.

His daughter looks back at him and smiles and the grandfather, for a moment, feels bathed in light. She turns away and he reaches for her shoulder. But the hand he raises is holding his drink and the other is holding her bag and both feel suddenly heavier. He weighs the cup in his palm and knows wistfully that the drink remains the best, most pleasure-giving thing he will experience that day, or the day after, or the day after that. He will see giraffes and he will hug his grandson and his daughter will smile at him and he will seize his mind on that orangutan cup and he will go to bed and he will wake up so he can have another. This is better than having no reason to wake up at all. After he flies home the months will pass until eventually his daughter will feel obligated to invite him for another visit, and he will feel obligated to go. He will hold his grandson every six or twelve months, and the boy will grow larger in his arms but remain impenetrable, and the Afghans will foist canned vegetables on him because they don't stock fresh. He will play Charlie Parker cassettes at night as he goes to sleep, and then lie alone in the large bed, missing his wife who had once had perfect breasts and is he such a terrible person for telling a joke about them at her wake? They had sex and enjoyed sex all forty-seven years of their marriage, and now he feels the need to tell someone this, but there is no one left who would want to hear it. He will take his orangutan cup with him on the plane, and sit at home watching CNN and sipping out of its domed head, and the act will remind him of his day at the zoo with his family.

The mother buckles her son into his car seat and her father sits next to him in the back. She looks at them in the rearview mirror as she pulls out of the parking lot. Her father has rested his hand on the boy's head. The hand just sits there, not patting or soothing or stroking, but it seems to calm the boy all the same. Her father takes a tissue from a box in the backseat and hands it to the boy. The boy pushes the tissue against his face, gluing it to his mucus-covered lip in an effort to please. The grandfather touches his cratered cheek, checking the square white bandage. He looks up and meets his daughter's eyes in the mirror. He is without a ready word, and his silence she is happy to interpret as love.

As the mother drives she ticks off what remains in the day to do. Dinner is taken care of. They can eat off paper plates so there are no dishes to wash. Her husband can play cribbage with her father while she tends to the boy. He needs a bath before bed. They will all watch the news and then sleep. Tomorrow she needs to be at work. Tomorrow she needs to telephone the mad scientist.

The Lion Gate

Renee watched the boy walk along the beach, thinking only of refusal. He was selling something towel to towel and whatever it was, she was sure she didn't want any. The boy was skinny and pale, with wild red hair and freckles. A spray of acne across his forehead made her feel sorry for him and then made her feel old. She guessed she was twice his age. He was handsome, despite the acne, despite his dirty T-shirt and cargo shorts and unzipped backpack leaking magazines and glue sticks. When he arrived at her towel, she draped a flowered beach-wrap over her still-pale thighs. Renee looked attractive without looking younger than she was, and most of the time she was proud of this.

He held a stack of handmade postcards, kaleidoscopic whirls of collaged Greek celebrities, headlines, ads. He shuffled through them and handed her a rose made of bikini tops and marble statues. "Send a card to the people back home?" he asked, in accentless American English. The stem of the rose was a single long leg. The thorns were high-heeled shoes, meticulously cut.

"Where are you from?" Renee asked, surprised.

"Boston. Cambridge."

"Pittsburgh."

"No way—mostly Germans and Italians here. Some dudes from UC-Davis at the hostel last week, but they left. Now it's just me. And you." He stared at Renee as if she were an exotic animal, precious and possibly endangered. "I'm Tick."

He asked how she'd ended up in Nafplio, and she started her story in the wrong place, too early, so that she thought she must be boring him, talking about her sabbatical from work, the years she'd fantasized about a trip to Greece. This was supposed to be the land of her lunch-hour romances, the novels of her airport layovers and waiting rooms: the strong-thighed women of Sparta, the oracles of Delphi, pledged to Apollo until strapping soldiers tested their resolve; the difficulty of courtship in the Late Helladic in their language without love letters, whose written form included only numbers and nouns. Linear B script was meant solely for inventories. In her favorite novel, an ingenious suitor managed to write his beloved a poem, a list of the gifts he would give her: *One woman, one gold bowl/One woman, one gold cup*.

She'd begun the trip staying in youth hostels because they seemed more adventurous, but the lounges were full of people like Tick, drinking Metaxa and strumming guitars and looking askance at her, the middle-aged woman who clearly didn't belong. In a youth hostel in Argos, the rooms were painted with large murals of drug paraphernalia. She slept in a bunk bed under a picture of a crooked hypodermic needle and thought: *I am too old for this. I am not old, but I am far too old for this.* A desk clerk had recommended Nafplio, a town sufficiently off the tourist trails that she could put the backpackers behind her and stay in a proper hotel without bankrupting herself.

She told Tick more of her story than she meant to, then stared down at the card. "Whose leg is this? Do you know?"

"Victoria Beckham. Posh Spice. I spray a latex glaze over the tops so the pictures won't fall off in the mail." He didn't offer his own travel story, but he gave her his full name, Ticknor Cody Whitworth. Renee laughed and then felt badly. "I'm named after George Ticknor," he explained. "He collected a lot of books and founded the Boston Public Library. My parents are professors."

Renee imagined what they might have intended, the well-scrubbed Ticknor who wielded a lacrosse stick for his East Coast school, wore polo shirts and got good grades. Tick's scrawniness seemed new, or temporary, his T-shirt sized for breadth he used to work at. He had been living out of a backpack for the last eight months, he said, on sandwiches and takeaways, and Renee offered to buy him dinner.

At the restaurant Renee was garrulous with wine, with the stored-up silence of a solo vacation. She spoke about the vanished boyfriend to whom she was not sending mail, about her discomfort with having, at age forty-three, only a *boyfriend,* about the many boyfriends Renee worried she'd squandered her twenties and thirties with. She'd kissed a lot of men and found no princes. Just frog, all frog. Or perhaps she'd kissed and discarded men who would have been, if not princes, allowable substitutes. She'd trawled through the frogs in her memory, holding her loneliness up against their perceived faults, wondering if it could have provided sufficient cover. She had resolved to be more forgiving, more patient, to entertain possibilities. Tick was not a prince, or a long-term solution—he was far too scruffy and broke and young—but he was, in the moment they kissed, something possible.

There were conversational topics to avoid: they could barely name ten of the same bands. As children they didn't play with the same toys or watch the same television shows. Renee talked about *Land of the Lost* and *H.R. Pufnstuf* and how a young Morgan Freeman gave phonics lessons on *The Electric Company.* Tick talked about *The Mighty Morphin Power Rangers.*

He was rewardingly curious, though, asking sincere questions about Renee's job in a dental practice. "I'm just the office manager," she said. "I don't have anything to do with the teeth."

"Not even the big plastic ones with eyes? Like you use to show kids how to brush?"

"We don't do pediatric. I get the catalogues, though. I could order you the *Adventures of Molaropolis,* Baron von Bitterbite vs. Mr. Mouth Guard."

Renee was joking but Tick said yes, order them now. He needed the *Adventures of Molaropolis.* He could not imagine not knowing what was going on in Molaropolis these days. He dragged the two of them to the Nafplio internet café to place an order.

Tick had surprisingly bad teeth. Renee couldn't help but notice. It was one more thing that made it impossible to imagine this happening back in Pittsburgh, her and Tick, Tick coming by the office to see her and all her coworkers asking each other, "Did you see his teeth?"

They spent nights drinking wine on the beach and then walked back to her hotel room, where Tick watched hours of Greek soap operas while she fell asleep. He almost never came to bed with her. Many nights he didn't seem to go to bed at all. Renee would wake up to find him still sitting on the floor, industriously decoupaging. On a few nights she woke up, disturbingly, to find him curled at the food of her bed sobbing. "What's wrong?" she asked, petting the length of his knobbed spine, but he wouldn't tell her. Other nights Renee woke to find him gone.

They tried a club together only once. Tick disappeared, leaving her for an hour with their two shots of ouzo. She finally got up to leave and spotted him dancing, his limbs flailing like a seizure, meeting her eye with a look not of guilt, but of absentminded pleasure, the surprised recognition of finding something he didn't realize he'd misplaced. Renee assumed that night he'd end up with someone younger, another tourist or a beautiful young Greek woman. Part of her thought this would be right and good and appropriate, however painful. But Tick returned to her, as he returned to her every night, even if the night was morning, the hotel laying out its continental breakfast. She opened the door and he offered her a bouquet of warm rolls. One morning he had a package: *The Adventures of Molaropolis* had arrived. Renee ate rolls in bed while Tick read aloud, doing different voices for Demi D. Kay and Ginger Vitus.

Tick brought her weed one night, and they smoked it in the dark on the beach. "H.R. Pufnstuf," Tick snorted, suddenly getting it. "Puff and stuff. Puff some stuff. Puff and—"

"H—R—Pufnstuf, who's your friend when things get rough? H—R—Pufnstuf—can't do a little 'cause he can't do enough." Renee sang the chorus of the old show, and Tick joined in on the reprise.

"You're much cooler than my parents," he told her.

"Oh God."

"I meant that as a compliment."

"I know you did. That's why I'm dying a little inside right now."

Renee was already embarrassed by how much she'd told him that first night at dinner, about the various frogs. She didn't dare say more about the most recent Frog, the one who said *someday* for years when she spoke of children; she was the one who'd broken it off, not because she no longer loved him, but because she was forty-three years old, and she was terrified that *someday* had become nearly *too late*. The ache she'd felt for the last two years at every baby on the bus, every child in the park, had sharpened to pain, reproachful and insistent. She could hear now the *someday* for what it had always been—*never, it's not what I want*—and blamed herself for forcing the Frog to lie, for allowing herself to hear only what she wanted. Newly single, she'd still been unsure what to do: fertility treatments, sperm donors, if they worked at all, could total tens of thousands of dollars her insurance wouldn't cover. Many adoption agencies wouldn't even consider her, a single woman at her age, and the ones that would needed $25,000 up front that she didn't have, years she wasn't sure she wanted to spend, reams of forms to fill out, all of them asking in different ways the obvious but undignified question of why, why wait so long, why do this alone? She didn't have enough money to buy herself a child, but she had enough for a trip. Perhaps, Renee had thought, she just needed some time away to help her make a decision. Perhaps the solution would present itself.

They visited the Palamidi Fortress that loomed over the city, a sweaty climb of 1000 steps to the top and achingly beautiful views of the Argolic Gulf. Renee read a pamphlet explaining that the fortress was erected by the Venetians in 1714. "Heh," Tick said. "Erected." On a weekday, the other visitors were mostly school groups. Renee walked by herself along the ramparts. When she returned to the courtyard Tick had infiltrated a snack break. Despite the lack of common language, he and some children had begun a mock battle between Venetians and Turks. Tick, leading the Ottomans, died extravagantly at the feet of a dark-haired girl, the mortal weapon of her pencil case buried between his elbow and side. A boy, excited by the heat of battle, kicked Tick hard in the ribs. Something in Tick flashed as he leapt, standing and looming over the boy. The child stepped back in surprise, almost fear. "Don't do that," Tick said. "Okay?"

"Okay," the boy parroted. The children were being corralled by their chaperones, but the boy stood long enough for Tick to stiffly clap a hand on his shoulder. Like father and son, Renee thought. Awkward father and obstreperous son. But still.

She made her proposal the next evening. Tick looked terrified. "A *baby*?" he said, his eyebrows high and eyes round and bloodshot. "With *me*?" They were in a restaurant, the other patrons looking studiously away.

"It would be—with you, but it wouldn't be with you. You wouldn't have to support us. We'd just go our separate ways."

"When?" Tick asked, and this was not the question Renee expected.

"When what?"

"When are we going our separate ways?"

"I don't know." Renee stabbed briefly at her spanakopita, answered his question with spinach in her mouth. "I have to be back at work at the end of September."

Tick did the math. "Oh," he said. "That's weeks away." He sounded relieved, and all of a sudden several weeks was all the time in the world, all of it anyone could want or need. He stared into his water glass. "So. You want a Baby Tick."

"I want a baby. I'd be honored to have you be the father," she added. "But I don't want you to feel creeped out. You don't have to really be a dad. I know how young you are. I'm sure you don't want that yet. But I'm ready, and I'd be so grateful if you'd help me."

Tick still looked confused more than anything, and Renee wanted for a moment to take it all back. She pictured a hyperactive infant with Tick's vertical red hair and angry skin and felt doubts unfurl.

"Why me?" Tick said, his eyebrows knit together, and Renee wondered, why him?

"You're smart," she said. "You're funny. You're nice, and you're good with kids. You like meeting new people. I've enjoyed spending time with you. And you're not bad looking." Renee enumerated Tick's many fine qualities until they were both very taken with this person, this Ticknor Whitworth, whom Renee thought so highly of.

"What if I wanted to? You know, be around. Play with the little guy. Or girl."

"Maybe," Renee said, and her immediate evasion surprised her. "I wouldn't want you to feel obligated."

"I wouldn't."

"I don't even know where you're going to be living, when you come back to the States. If you come back."

"I could come to Pittsburgh," Tick said, and Renee smiled tightly.

"How about you just think about the one thing," she said. "Before you think about the other. How about you just decide on whether or not you're willing to—help me. Just that for now. And maybe Pittsburgh we talk about later."

Back at the hotel Tick showered, and climbed under the sheets smelling like hotel soap, his skin and hair still damp. He reminded her of something very fresh and new, like a plate still steaming from the dishwasher or a fluffy load of laundry. He had trouble that night in bed. Renee assumed that their conversation at dinner was distracting him, but it wasn't the first time Tick had had this problem. Renee couldn't help but take it personally however often Tick told her not to. He'd told her that she was beautiful, she was sexy. Told her that it was all him, just some stuff he'd been going through, nothing to do with her at all. His erections could flag quickly, especially as they paused for a condom. Sometimes he softened inside her. "Would it be better for you without?" Renee asked that night.

Tick paused, stilled. "If you want."

He didn't really seem to care, and Renee was a little offended. They traded standard assurances, that they were free of disease, that nothing terrible would come of whatever they decided.

"Then go without," she said, and he just nodded. He didn't ask if she was on the pill. She expected to have the opportunity to tell him that she wasn't using anything, hadn't since she and the Frog broke up. She'd planned on seeing how he reacted. But because he didn't ask, she felt strange announcing it. Renee wasn't sure in that moment that Tick was even thinking about their conversation in the restaurant. But he did as she suggested, and Renee was unwilling to stop him.

Afterward, Tick slept, and Renee watched his still face, his closed eyes. He looked strangely beautiful in a fragile way, like Greek statuary reduced to a head or a torso and a placid, immovable expression. "Tick," Renee whispered, and when he didn't move said, "Tock." She put her hand in his hair and tugged it gently back and forth. "Tick tock," she said. It was so rare that she saw him sleep. He looked very vulnerable. He made her want to do something for him, although she was not sure what that might be. He looked like he needed something, and she didn't know what.

He was in the bathroom when the phone rang the next morning. It was an American voice on the other end, a woman. "Do you know a boy named Ticknor Whitworth?" she asked.

A *boy,* Renee thought. Tick as a *boy.* There was a long pause.

"This is his mother."

"Oh." Renee was startled, reluctant to announce that Tick was in the shower, with all that implied about their relationship. "I can have him call you."

"Is he all right?"

"He's fine. Is there a problem?"

"I just need to make sure he's okay. I lost track of him after Corfu. When his friends left. One of them called from Dubrovnik. They said he was scaring them. I don't know what they should have done. They said they thought they could send a message by leaving."

"I don't know what you're talking about."

"I believe they thought it was the right thing to do."

"Professor Whitworth," Renee said, because the woman's occupation was the sole thing she knew about her. Renee paused when she heard how ridiculous it sounded, as if she were enrolled in a difficult class and needed help with the material.

"Ava," Mrs. Whitworth said. "It's Ava, please."

"Tick was already in town when I got here. He's been on the mainland for weeks."

"I've been calling all the hostels. He told someone in Patrai that he was headed to Nafplio. The hostel there said he'd moved to the Pension Dioscouri. I described him to your desk clerk. She said she couldn't give the number but she'd connect me. She said he was staying there with an older woman. She said you were a dentist."

Renee wondered what Mrs. Whitworth was picturing. What was "an older woman"? Than Tick, almost anyone.

"I had an extra bed," Renee lied. "And the local hostel's pretty down at heel. He was traveling on a budget, and I thought I might as well offer."

"I'm glad someone's looking after him," Ava said, not without suspicion in her voice, and Renee wondered if what she was doing with Tick could be called looking after.

"Is he still using?" Ava asked, and Renee almost answered "Using what?" before her throat clamped closed in the rush of recognition. Of course. Of course of course of course. The lightning of him, the flint and the spark. The frantic energy and confusion and the way he was too old to act so young, too young to look so ragged, his graying teeth and angry skin. Renee's face flamed; below her stomach her insides clenched, as if last night was something her body could disallow. Ava took her silence as confirmation.

"I'm glad you're there. You're making sure he eats?"

Renee nodded, said yes. She was making sure Tick ate. She was doing that much.

"Can you tell him to check his email? I've written him—I don't know how many times I've written him."

"I'll try."

"What's your name?" The woman's voice was suddenly sharp and needy.

"Renee."

"Are you a mother, Renee?"

She was silent. The water shut off in the bathroom. "I have to go."

"Let me give you my number. It's a new cell phone. Can you give it to him? As a mother, I'm asking you. Please help send him home."

As the woman recited the number, Renee jotted it down automatically on the hotel notepad. The bathroom door began to open, and Renee hung up without making any promises, any plans, without comforting the woman or saying goodbye.

Tick emerged, flushed and wrapped in a towel. "What?" he asked when he saw her staring. "Enjoying the view?"

Renee's left hand was still hovering by the phone, her right still holding the pen.

"Who were you talking to?"

"Nobody. The front desk."

"You made notes."

"It's—a number we're supposed to call if we have any complaints. A customer satisfaction thing." Renee ripped the page from the notebook. "You have any complaints?"

"Nope." Tick frowned slightly as she folded the note tightly into halves, quarters, eighths. "You'd better get ready, if we're going to make that bus you wanted."

Renee nodded, stood and carried the note with her into the bathroom.

Every gesture, every possible conversation, felt more difficult than simply going through the motions of the day. She packed her sightseeing bag: camera, water bottle, sunscreen. She added a book and pulled it out as soon as they took their seats on the bus. When Tick saw that she wasn't going to be any fun, he put earphones in, loud music seeping murkily out, and played a complicated tapping game with his own fingers. The bus was largely empty, and a few old women gave them odd looks, these mismatched strangers who could have their own seats.

The book, her favorite, was too familiar to be a distraction. Renee anticipated the plot points, the suitor's suspicion that his lover had been unfaithful: *One woman, a hundred snakes/ One woman, a thousand piles of garbage,* he wrote her, while the woman groped for the nouns that could vindicate her. Finally the suitor came rushing back, a handmaid having snuck away to tell him the truth. This part had never bothered her before, but now she felt cheated at the omissions. She needed to know what the handmaid had found to say, what single speech had rescued them all. "Tick," she whispered, as curious as anyone to know what her next words might be. With his earphones in, he didn't hear her. He was playing air-drums with a pencil and a tube of chapstick, his eyes closed.

They toured the Sanctuary of Asklepios, where ancient Greeks once brought their illnesses to the gods of healing. There was a temple where the afflicted spent the night and hoped to dream their cures, to wake up knowing how to solve themselves. Tick wandered off and Renee walked the old foundations in a daze. The sun was climbing, the day already hot, and Renee sat with her back against a boulder. Nothing had changed, she tried to tell herself. Tick was always Tick; she was just seeing him now in his proper light. Ava Whitworth's phone number was a stone in her pocket. Renee knew what she was supposed to do—place it in Tick's palm and curl his fingers over it, urge him to call his family and get the help he needed. Instead she lowered herself onto the dirt and flagstones, spread her arms out against the warm ground and pointed her toes. She could just lie there, she thought, until her child-hunger faded to a murmur, to something impossible and half-remembered. She could wait until Tick had crashed or somehow gotten sober, bad enough or well enough to go home on his own, no longer her responsibility. She could lie there until all her choices were gone and Asklepios appeared to her bones to take credit for the cure. A tour group approached and then faded down another route. She asked her body, part by part, whether anything felt different, flaring with infection or improbable life. The reports came in from her flexed toes and fingers, from her nervous stomach and lower, from the cradle of her hips and between her legs. No, they said. Probably not, they said. It was a single night, they said, and she felt emptier than ever, her body stripped even of the possibility of disaster. She should be changed, and all she was was humiliated. She thought dark words about Ava Whitworth, who was granted a child and managed to misplace him like a lost suitcase, delivered accidentally to Renee's doorstep.

A single set of footsteps came closer and she opened her

eyes. Tick was standing above her. He noticed her squinting in the sun and leaned forward, his body shading her. "You okay?" he asked.

"Just fine. You?"

Tick shrugged.

They took another bus to Mycenae, the next stop on their planned itinerary. They traced the upper Acropolis and the Cyclopean walls. All just piles of stones. They looked out at the dry, yellow hills, planted with orderly rows of olive trees. They stood among the ruins and decided they were ready to go. The day felt very long.

They consulted the bus times listed in the guidebook but waited at the stop nearly an hour. There was a tiny post office kiosk in the parking lot where the clerk made them buy something, a single stamp, before she explained that the buses had switched to new off-season schedules. It was September, the woman said, and the next bus to Nafplio wouldn't leave for nearly three hours.

"Let's go back up to the site, I guess," Tick said. He licked their stamp and stuck it to his forehead.

"You could have used that," Renee said.

"I am using it."

"To send mail. I was going to buy you a postcard. You never write to anyone."

"I make cards. I don't want more."

They walked up the wide stone ramp, through the Lion Gate back into the heart of the old citadel, where Tick read from the guidebook to pass the time. He wriggled his butt onto a comfortable rock, announced, "I have gazed upon the ass groove of Agamemnon." He put names to the heaps of stone Renee had no patience for, the storeroom of the archers and the temple of Hera. "Listen to this," he perked up. "Apparently there's 'an underground cistern, approached by a long flight of uneven, unlit stone steps, ending in an abrupt five meter drop into icy water. While not explicitly off-limits to tourists, the descent is discouraged for obvious reasons. Anyone considering it should be equipped with a good flashlight and take the proper precautions.'"

He looked at Renee until she shrugged, aware she was disappointing him.

"What are we doing still sitting around here?" Tick asked rhetorically.

"The pitch-dark, five-meter drop and icy water are three reasons I'm still sitting here."

"Come on," Tick urged. "Where's your sense of adventure? We've got ages 'til the bus."

This convinced Renee, this reminder that unless they descended into the cistern, they would have to make hours of conversation.

They didn't have a flashlight, and there weren't any for sale in the parking lot souvenir stand. They took Renee's camera out of the backpack and tested the flash. In the daylight, it looked feeble. They found the entrance marked on the guidebook map, a simple stone doorframe leading down into blackness. Renee felt a shiver of excitement; American tourist attractions would never allow such danger, such palpable potential harm.

There was the awkwardness of deciding who would go first, when Tick took her camera and held it in front of him. "I'll protect you," he said. "My Lady of Mycenae."

Renee stretched her arm in front of her and took his shoulder like a blind woman as they descended. Tick took a picture of nothingness and in the flash, fading as soon as it burst, they shuffled forward. The steps were uneven and worn smooth. Renee slipped once and nearly knocked them both over. The flash illuminated only a foot or two ahead and in the darkness the flash blinded as much as it helped. Renee wasn't sure how much battery-life was left in the camera. "Do you think we should turn back?" she asked.

"No way," Tick said with sincerity, but he paused in the dark. Renee could feel his shoulder lowering the camera. They listened to the darkness, to the sound of their breath. It felt like they had been descending forever. Tick reached back with one arm and took her hand. His palm was soft and warm, slightly damp, and Renee was filled with tenderness. There was nothing else. No light, no sound. No burble of water. Then the mechanical click and wheeze of light, and the next stumble forward, the lengthening and closing of their joined arms as they descended together.

Then the flash illuminated a blank stone wall.

"The hell?" Tick said, and pulled his hand away, triggering the flash over and over until Renee grabbed his arm.

"They've sealed it off." She held his hand and they rotated in a tight circle, illuminating the squared-off edges of a small landing, bricked on three sides by solid stone.

"It isn't here," he said, sounding shocked.

"Or it's been drained, and we've been walking down into where the water used to be." Renee was disappointed but relieved.

"It isn't here," Tick repeated, and continued to flash the camera in a circle. "It was supposed to be here. The book said it would be here. It's supposed to be here," Tick chanted.

"So they changed it," Renee said. "It's okay."

Tick fumbled the camera, his fingers illuminated as they groped at the falling flash. Renee heard the camera hit the ground, then the sound of what she thought was Tick kicking it against the bottom of the stairs. "Tick," she said, scolding.

"It isn't fucking fair," he wailed. She could hear the flat, thin percussion of skin against stone, his hands, she assumed, slapping the walls. "Tick, stop," she said, and said it again, as the sound continued. "Stop!" she yelled, when she heard a dull, rounder sound, what she was terrified was the thud of his forehead against rock. She got her arms around him and managed to turn him and push him down the wall. She was grateful that he was so thin. She slid herself behind him, her legs spread to fit around his hips. He tensed, then leaned his head against her shoulder. She stroked his hair with her right hand, held him tightly across the ribcage with her left. Eventually he was quiet. She curved a palm on his forehead and felt a strange, smooth square. The postage stamp, she remembered.

"Renee?" Tick finally whispered.

"Yes?"

"I don't want to be a dad," he said. "I don't think it's a good idea."

"Oh Tick." She pressed her right temple against his left and they breathed together. His skin was damp. "It isn't, is it? I shouldn't have asked. I shouldn't have ever asked you."

"Sorry," he said.

She drew both arms firmly around him and felt him shake. "I'm sorry," she said, and meant it. "I'll think of something else," she said, and meant that too. She said it for herself, not Tick, and hearing it aloud she believed that she would. Her legs ached, spread on the hard ground. She stretched them out farther and her toes brushed the front edge of the bottom step. She was comforted by the stairway now, that in the dark it offered them a direction, a single possibility. She held Tick tighter and rocked him. "Are you ready to go home now?" she asked. She listened to his body for an answer. She listened to her own.

In a moment, they would rise and go.

This Is Not Your City

Nika is missing. Her daughter is missing, and there are two policemen in Daria's kitchen. She does not know what to say to them. "Do you want coffee?" she asks, her voice cracking on the upswing of the question. It is one of the only perfect sentences she knows, one of the first she learned. The policemen shake their heads, and Daria's husband Paavo makes it understood that he will answer their questions, sign their forms. He lifts his fingers curled around an invisible pen and signs his name with a flourish on the air. Daria goes to sit on Paavo's bed. Missing is better than it could be. Paavo had groped for the word in his dictionary. The policemen looked embarrassed for them, and Daria remembered why she did not usually open the door to strangers. The first entry Paavo pointed to meant gone, and Daria almost died. It was several minutes, terrible gestures, the younger policeman with his hand like a visor on his forehead, pretending to look for her daughter under the cupboards, until Daria understood as much as she did.

She has left the kitchen still holding Paavo's dictionary. They each have one, pocket-sized, with a larger one on the bookshelf in the living room. They have not needed the big one yet; their conversation is not so complex. She turns to *dead* in Russian and rips out the page. She will eat it, she thinks, like an old-time spy, so no one can bring her bad news. She thinks

137

she is joking to herself until she takes a bite of the upper-right corner. She chews and swallows, creases the page in half, tears a bite from the middle. She unfolds it and holds it up in front of the window. It is late evening, but the sun is still up. She washed and bleached the curtains a week ago and admires through the paper how white they are now. The page is soft but substantial, good to chew. It has a flat taste like raw oats. She realizes that Paavo would not need this page to tell her that her daughter is dead. He would turn, of course, to the Finnish, and Daria has already swallowed the translation so she does not know what word to rip out. She eats the rest of the Russian page anyway.

Daria hears the policemen leave, and Paavo comes into the bedroom, gestures for his dictionary. He sits on the edge of the bed with a pencil and pad of paper, and Daria is relieved that he doesn't notice the missing page. He looks studious, reading glasses pushed down his nose as he writes things out for her, his Cyrillic letters as misshapen as a child's. Nika and Matti, her boyfriend, have not come back from their camping trip. They were due in the morning at Matti's house to return the car and were going to spend the day there. All day Matti's mother tried to call his cell phone. All day nothing, and at dinnertime she called the police. A Russian interpreter will be by tomorrow morning, to explain things better, to ask Daria some questions. Daria nods.

Nika is still missing, and Daria still does not know what to do, so she heats the sauna. She strips off her clothes and lets them sit in a heap on the bathroom floor. She fills the red plastic bucket with cold water and pulls the ladle from its peg on the wall. Paavo is always saying he will buy birch, a proper bucket and scoop, but Daria doesn't care. She heats the sauna hotter than she ever has before and dumps water on the rocks until sweat runs into her eyes and they hurt so badly it's okay if she cries. The steam is searing. She has left her earrings in and she can feel the silver getting hotter, drawing the burn up through the hooks into her ears. They will blister if she leaves them, burn her fingers if she takes them out. She tugs them quickly from her ears and lets them drop between the pine boards to the floor.

When she steps out into the bathroom her eyes are sore and so salted she can barely see. She wraps a towel around herself and walks to the bedroom. Paavo is sitting on the bed watching television, duvet over his legs, his chest bare. He has an old man's body, with small, pointy breasts, white hairs curling around the nipples. Skinny legs and arms, a great melon of a belly. His hair is gray but thick, with a swoop above his forehead; he is not so very old, yet.

"Are you okay?" he asks.

"No. Yes." She mimes sweating, rubs her eyes, says "ouch." Paavo nods, willing as ever to be lied to.

"Sauna. Still hot. If you want," she says.

Paavo shakes his head. Daria wonders if her body is still hot enough to scald him, wonders what damage she could do if she reached for him now. Paavo turns the channel from Formula One highlights, looking for something he thinks she will like better. He stops at an old episode of *Friends* and Daria listens to the laugh track. Someday, she thinks, if she grows old in this country, she will know by herself what's so funny. She has seen this episode already, back at home in Vyborg, the voices dubbed. Chandler is inside a box on the floor, apologizing. She recognizes this much, his apology, and she realizes it is a word that Finnish people never speak aloud. *Excuse me* they say easily, but never this, *olen pahoillani*, a sad man locked in a box. She wonders if Nika knows this word yet, *pahoillani*, if she could say it in their new language and be understood. *Olen pahoillani. Tyttäreni.* I'm sorry. My daughter, I'm sorry.

Daria puts on her nightgown and joins Paavo in the bed, he under his comforter, she under hers. She lies on her side, facing away from her husband. She hears him turn the television off and put the remote on the nightstand. He puts his hand on her shoulder, and she is waiting for it to trail lower, down her spine or over the curve of her hip, when instead he touches her hair. He pets her head like a child's. "It will be all right," he says, and Daria is grateful, but somehow lonelier. Sex is a language they can pretend to have in common; he grunts, he waits for her to sigh, and they can imagine that they understand each other. She doesn't like it when Paavo talks in bed. Her ears know he is a stranger, and if he spoke while he touched her, her skin would know it, her bones would know it, her sex would know that she has agreed to spend her life in a stranger's bed.

The agency promised her no better. She has not been cheated. You have a daughter, they told her. Fourteen years old. What do you expect us to find for you? A divorcée, no less, which seemed to imply to the matchmakers a lack of fortitude, fatally unrealistic expectations. Her first husband did not beat her, she had been forced to admit to them. He was drunk only on weekends when he was in Vyborg, which was only two weeks out of every sixteen. He went to the oil fields in Western Siberia, and brought home money, and how could she be so dissatisfied with someone who was not even there? You wouldn't understand, she said to them. It is what she has been saying for nine years, and what started as reluctance to unburden herself to nosy aunts and cousins has in those nine years become something true. She has forgotten why she staked her hopes on something better, something different, why she was so sure of success. Daria knows that if she thinks about the divorce too long she will be forced to admit that she would not do it again. It is a monstrous realization that she has made a mistake of that magnitude with her life, something that cannot be mended or taken back. If she could choose again she would stay, and it seems like the worst thing she could know about herself.

If she had stayed, she might never have had to go to work at the Vyborg market hall, the building by the bay that still has *Kauppahalli* inscribed in cement above the main doors. In the years after the war, her parents told her, thousands of such signs were scratched out, repainted, re-hung. The statelier ones, letters cut into granite or marble, have stayed. So she knows the Finnish for *market hall*, for *train station*, for *bank*. She also knows the Finnish for *chocolates*, and *taste*, and *very inexpensive*, the words she used behind the broad table at the back wall, plastic bins of foil-wrapped candies before her. The teenager at the next table sold bootleg CDs and taught her to recognize the Finns. Terrible clothes and stylish glasses, he told her. Jogging suits and sharp dark frames. That's the look of money.

Daria thinks she will not sleep this night, the sky a starless waking blue, but hours later she finds herself stirring, groggy, the early light pale and confused. When Paavo wakes she has porridge ready, homemade and heavy, a pool of black currant jam in the middle of the bowl. He manages to ask her if she wants him to stay home from work. "Go," she tells him. Paavo works at the pulp factory, and the smell of him after a shift is the smell of the air over the town, the wind off the lake; it smells something like stewed cabbage, and the townspeople have only one joke about it. Smell that, they say, noses in the air. The scent of money. On good days the breeze comes from the other end of the lake, where the Japanese have built a new sawmill. That smell reminds Daria of the forest near Ladoga, picking at bark with her fingernails and opening a divot that bled sap and the pine scent of the tree. She told this to Nika one day when the wind was good, and Nika rolled her eyes. "It's a sawmill, Mom. That's the smell of dead trees. Dead trees getting chopped into little bits."

Not little bits, Daria thinks, not unless the grain is bad. She knows the trees she smells are being planed into boards, long and straight and someday someone's home. But they are dead all the same. She must grant her daughter that, and to explain the rest seems like so much effort. Nika is fifteen now and does not like to listen.

While Daria waits for the interpreter, she cleans the kitchen. She cleans the venetian blinds slat by slat because she cannot figure out how to unhook them from the window frame. The thin panels are sharper than they look, and she cuts her fingers in three places. She leaves a streak of blood on a slat close to the ceiling. She likes hiding a part of herself in the apartment, as if it is a claim to the space, a promise that she will not have to leave it, although her entire life has taught her otherwise. She was born in a city that once spoke another language. She thinks the Finns who visited came only to be angry; they kicked the dissolving sidewalks like the tires of an old car they would have taken better care of. This is not your city anymore, she wanted to tell them. It has not been your city for fifty years. Leave us alone.

Daria scrubs the stovetop and wonders if the translator will be a Russian-speaking Finn, or the other way round. She wonders whether to make tea sweetened with jam, or the endless cups of coffee her husband drinks. The doorbell rings and Daria's heart is frantic. Through the peephole there is only a sour-looking man, older than she is, younger than Paavo. "Daria Kikkunen?" he says when she opens the door, and she nods. She listens to his accent and makes them coffee. The interpreter asks her about Nika and Matti, about their weekend plans. Daria is embarrassed at how little she knows. Only the backpack Nika filled, the sleeping bag she borrowed from Paavo and complained smelled like an old man, smoke and aftershave. The borrowed car to drive north of Kuusamo, to celebrate the midsummer weekend.

The interpreter asks about Matti, and Daria tells him what she knows, how one night four months ago they were all sitting in the living room when a car pulled to a stop outside and honked its horn. "Poikaystäväni," Nika announced in Finnish, "my boyfriend," took her coat from the hallway closet and left. Nika cannot speak the language, had at that time been in the country for all of eight weeks; what kind of a boyfriend could she have? The interpreter gives Daria an ugly look, but leans closer, his hands stretching over his notepad and pen, his sleeves sweeping the table. Daria leans back without thinking, then asks herself why she is bothering to be afraid of this man, balding, his skin the white-yellow of new potatoes. Daria tells him that she has seen Matti a few times, that she remembers a boy like a great gold mastiff, giant and eager and mysteriously happy. Dog-boy, Daria says to herself, although she is forced to admit he is handsome in a way that seems terribly young.

Nika thinks they have never spoken, her boyfriend and her mother, only nodded at each other from the apartment door as she comes or goes. Nika does not know that six weeks ago they ran into each other in the Prisma parking lot. Daria remembers being surprised when she left the store that evening and there was still light in the sky. A cold wind, but a portion of sun: signs of spring. Matti and Daria recognized each other and said "hello," cleared their throats, shifted their feet. Then Matti said, "Nika is a very nice girl." He said it slowly and clearly, and she understood him. He said it a little loudly, too, which embarrassed her, but she could see he was trying. "I like her very much. Do you understand?" he asked, and Daria nodded. "I can take—" he said, pointing at her shopping bags, and before she could protest he'd lifted them out of her arms and begun to walk toward Paavo's car. He waited while she unlocked the trunk and then put them down carefully. He handed her the plastic bag with the eggs, and Daria was surprised that he would think to do that. She was surprised that he seemed such a decent boy, so surprised, in fact, that she felt guilty for her astonishment. He took her hand, held it for a moment. "It is good," he said. "That you bring her. That you bring Nika here. It is a happy thing."

Daria knew he was speaking like a child for her, but even so, whatever he said next slipped past her. She smiled anyway, pressed his hand between hers. It was something about "happy," about a "good life," about "welcome." It was something that, standing there in the Prisma parking lot with a beautiful boy as cheerful as a golden retriever, she could convince herself would someday be true.

"He's a decent boy," Daria tells the interpreter. "Truly. Better than I thought."

The interpreter seems impatient, a man who learned her language thinking it would be of more importance than it has turned out to be. The language of diplomacy has turned into the language of sad women in kitchens and too-sweet tea. He asks for her patronymic, and Daria doesn't know if he wants to address her properly in Russian or simply be intrusive, make her reveal a name she no longer has any use for, a person she no longer is. Daria Fedorovna, he says, tell me about your daughter, and for a moment Nika feels like someone else's child. The interpreter eats four slices of pulla, one after another. It isn't homemade, but he compliments her anyway. Daria pulls more pastry from the bag and slices it finer, fans it out on the plate. She pours him another cup of coffee.

Nika hadn't wanted to leave, Daria confesses. There was her school, her home, her whole life. There had been a boy. He was twenty and worked in the post office. Nika was fourteen. Daria forbade her to see him, and Nika laughed at her. Now in this country Nika looks too old, eighteen instead of fifteen, but in Finnish she speaks like a child. I don't want. I do. Yes,

I like cigarette. Daria is scared that Nika, too, will end up in a stranger's bed, and if that happens this will have been for nothing.

"Do you think she might have tried to go back?" the interpreter asks her, and Daria doesn't know. It seems so monumentally stupid, a kick in the teeth to her mother, to the marriage. It seems like something, on second thought, Nika might have decided to do. But when Daria looks in Paavo's filing cabinet Nika's passport is still there. She shows it to the interpreter. One page has Nika's visa glued in, another is stamped Nuijamaa, where Paavo drove his new wife and daughter across the border for the first and last time in a Ford Fiesta. "It looks the same," Nika had announced, crossing into Finland. For thirty kilometers of nothing but forest she was right. The towns, though. Even the villages. So tidy and glossy, pasteurized to the blue-white of skim milk. It was a long drive, and at the end of it was a town so small, so far from the border, it had none of the amenities the agency had suggested she look for: no language classes, no foreign social clubs, no international center where she could sit with other Russian mothers and discuss ways to save their children.

The interpreter thanks her for her time, when it is clear that it is his own that he feels has been wasted. The pad he brought to take notes is mostly empty. She shows him out and then stands on the balcony, watching him unlock his car and drive off. The green on the trees is still pale, the birches fluffy with light-veined leaves. It was a long winter, and patches of snow stayed slumped in the shade of the pine trees until May. Now Daria has not seen stars for weeks, and she does not miss them. She has put potted plants all along the edges of the balcony, some balanced on the railing and tied precariously with twine to the rungs, and in the long summer light they are finally starting to grow. The blue nights husband the herbs, the vegetables, which they will have fresh and now not so expensively. The supermarkets here make her nervous. It is sometimes a physical pain, to pay so much for things. In the register lines she sweats and brings the groceries home with damp patches under her arms.

Daria looks in the cupboards, plans dinner. She takes steaks from the freezer to thaw. It is too early to do anything else and the apartment is not big enough to occupy her with cleaning. She did the living room and Paavo's bedroom only yesterday, when Nika was already missing but her mother did not even know. So Daria turns the handle of Nika's door. Her daughter has learned at least one thing in Finnish: *Pääsy Kielletty*. She has written it in black marker on a piece of notebook paper and taped it to her door. No Entry.

Nika's room is a glorious mess, alive with her daughter's things, the smell of her, the perfume Daria suspects she stole, the floor shining with the glitter Nika glues to her eyelids with Vaseline. The top of the dresser is littered with makeup, a dark purple lipstick worn away at a sloping angle, a black eyeliner as blunted as a crayon. Nika wears thick streaks of it every day, doesn't wash it off at night, comes out of her bedroom in the morning looking like a sluggish raccoon. Daria wants to tell her that she must always take off her makeup, that to leave it on will someday make her look ten years older. She wants to tell Nika a thousand things, and practices speeches to her daughter in her head so often they are threadbare before she has the courage to say them aloud, as if struggling so hard in one language has made her mute in every other.

The marriage is a gaping hush, an unraveling hole that cannot be darned. It is growing. It has swallowed the girl Daria was, who spun terrible fairy tales in her school notebooks, about princesses and white horses and the blood-pricked thorns of roses, the icy shards of hearts. It has swallowed the woman Daria was who narrated her days. Who said, this is what happened today. This is who I saw. This is what we talked about. This is who has gotten fat. It has swallowed the woman who asked, how was school today?—and worse, the silence has swallowed the daughter who sometimes answered her. Daria has sold herself for nothing, because her daughter is becoming as mute as she is. How was school today, she says in Russian, and Nika has no answer, not in any language, not in the one she was born with, or in the three she is supposed to be learning. Not in Finnish, or the English she takes three times a week, or the Swedish she is required to take for two, another language she cannot speak, another she does not need, another class she will fail. Paavo has had to put his signature on Swedish tests turned in blank, Nika's name written on the top and every question unanswered. Can't you try harder, Daria has asked her. How do you still know nothing? Speak, Daria has begged her. Just speak. Please.

If Nika writes fairy tales, she has never shown them to her mother. Math was her best subject in Vyborg, and in Outojärvi it is one of the only ones she passed. Her marks would be perfect except for the word problems lurking at the end of every exam. Sometimes she reads them well enough to solve, and those tests Daria sticks to the refrigerator. Nika is a practical child, and has never, as her mother once did secretly, rhymed storm clouds as dark as her soul, or a love that burned like fire. It is just as well, Daria thinks, because the love Daria has known has never burned like fire, and her heart has never broken into shards. It simply beats and that is a language of its own, useless and irrefutable. The heart has one word only, and however wrong or right her life might have gone it would have the one word still.

Daria scoops clothes from Nika's floor into a hamper, puts tissues blotted with lipstick into the wastebasket. The school year ended three weeks ago, and Nika's schoolbooks are in a pile in the corner, where she dumped them to empty her backpack for camping. Daria stacks them neatly. Nika's grade report recommended she repeat the year. Paavo said he'd talk to the headmaster again, meet with the teachers, see what he could do. He did not sound hopeful.

"It's okay," Nika shrugged.

"Don't you want to keep up with your friends?" Daria asked, in Russian.

"What friends?" Nika said, then added, because she could, "Matti's graduating anyway."

"And doing what?"

"Looking for work. Staying in town."

"What kind of work?"

"Why do you care? You sold candy. You don't work at all now."

"I work."

"Being Paavo's wife? I guess that's work. I guess that's some kind of work," Nika said, and Daria blushed.

∞

Beneath the stack of Nika's school things there is a folder Daria recognizes, a packet of "Helpful Hints" from the agency. Phrases for courtship, for proposals, for visa arrangements and a life together in two languages: *You are very beautiful. I believe strongly in good family life. My hobbies are to bake and cook. I am sincere and passionate. I like fidelity.*

One of Daria's friends with a PhD in Comparative Literature and a job managing a florist shop had read it over and laughed. "Full of mistakes. You memorize these and you'll sound even stupider."

The agency had already drawn up Daria's profile with a "1" under language skills: Some basic phrases. Cannot write or talk on telephone.

Daria doesn't understand why Nika would have this folder until she turns a page and reads Nika's notes. There are pages of endearments she has practiced writing over and over, until her handwriting is not so awkward. She has copied phrases out on blank pages to memorize them, inserted Matti's name on the blank lines. *I want to give you the world. Can you speak slower? My heart is like a bird that is ready to zoom up to the sky. Am I deserving for your love?*

"Sexy," the agency had told her. "These pictures are not sexy."

Daria had borrowed a camera from a friend and asked Nika to go with her to a city park near their apartment. Nika's pictures were headshots, Daria leaning against tree trunks and smiling to show off her straight teeth, shiny brown hair, careful makeup that you could see she did not really need. Daria had Nika when she was twenty-two, was thirty-six when she signed up with the agency. Not so old. She has never smoked and her skin is good for her age, mostly unlined.

"You can't even see your body in these. Who will be interested? They'll think you're fat and trying to hide it."

Daria is slim, almost skinny. She is proud that she does not eat much, that she could wear her daughter's clothes if she wanted to.

"What do you think the men will be looking for? Why do

you think they'll pick you? Your teenage daughter? Your "1" in language? We need other photos."

Daria asked Nika to take those photos, too, in her bedroom with the blinds pulled down. Their apartment had only two rooms—Daria slept on the couch in the living room. To be on a bed it had to be Nika's—to wear sexy clothes, those were mostly Nika's, too. There was the shot of her on her hands and knees on the bed, in a short robe, barely covered. The shot she leaned over for, her cleavage at the center of the picture. It was one of Nika's bras that gave the best effect, a padded purple one that pushed Daria's small breasts up and together. Daria knew the bra from doing the laundry and asked to try it.

"Maybe your purple one. That might look best."

"Mom."

"Please. I need you to help me with this. I'll wash it for you after, if you want. It'll be dry by tomorrow morning if you want to wear it."

"Mom."

"Please," Daria had begged her daughter, and Nika had done it. She had fished her bra out of her dresser, pulled her shortest skirts from the closet, the shirts with the lowest necklines. Daria tried to think of the clothes only as costume changes, a whirl of scenery and props as her daughter positioned her in the doorway, on the bed, the nightstand lamp on and then off. She lay on her back, her arms over her head, one leg bent; Nika slit open the blinds and striped her mother with sunlight. "Maybe undo another button," Nika said. "Pull it down a little. Pull the shoulders wide."

The shirt was one Nika had begged for before her first day of high school; she'd bargained for the bra when it went on sale at a department store. The skirt had been a reward when Nika scored highest in her class on a trigonometry exam.

"Do you think this is sexy enough?" Daria kept saying, hating herself but having no one else to ask.

"You're sexy. The pictures will be sexy. Stop worrying," Nika told her. She bent and shaped her mother's limbs like a doll's rubber legs, crooked plastic arms. She lifted a skirt higher on Daria's thighs, the hem pinched between her thumb and middle finger. Daria could feel the tongue of her daughter's fingers not-touching her as the fabric settled over her skin.

"Much better," the agency told them. "Much," and at the time Daria was relieved. Yet if she had to put her finger on the moment it started to spread, the toothed silence between them, she would probably mark it there, that Sunday afternoon in Nika's bedroom with the blinds drawn, Daria dressed in her daughter's underwear. It was a long time before Nika wore those clothes again. The purple bra did not turn up in the wash for weeks. But Nika did not have so many clothes she could afford to be that choosy, and eventually they all showed up again, the skirts and shirts and the short robe. Her clothes are one more way that Nika has not fit in here, but she has refused new ones. Nika and Daria both know that Paavo disapproves. He has copied down Nika's size from the tags inside her clothes and bought her loose jeans and sweaters. She wears them most often when he is not around.

There is the sound of a car outside, and Daria wonders if the day has sped forward so quickly, that Paavo is home already. In June the light changes so little that it is hard to tell the time. Daria wakes sometimes at four a.m. and doesn't know if it's time to get up and make breakfast or to go back to sleep. She wakes sometimes with Paavo holding her, and when she tries to get up, he tells her again that he does not need a cooked breakfast, that bread and cheese and yogurt did him fine for years, they will do him fine now, that he does not need the things she thinks she owes him.

Daria puts Nika's notebook back under the stack of schoolbooks, arranges them so it will not look like she was spying. She is already worried to be here in Nika's room, to have picked up her laundry. Daria can taste the fight they will have about it when Nika comes home. When. There is a key unlocking the front door, and Daria stands with the hamper on her hip. She does not want Paavo to see Nika's room, to criticize the mess. But it is not Paavo who has unlocked the front door, who walks down the hall to the bedroom.

"You're in my room," Nika says.

Daria drops the laundry and takes her daughter in her arms. She has not had the courage to hold her daughter this desperately since Nika turned eleven and started practicing surly looks in the bathroom mirror. Daria holds her now and rocks her back and forth on their feet. She is taller than her daughter, and holds her so hard that Nika is standing on her toes before her mother lets her down and looks at her. Nika's hair is pulled back tight, in a fierce but messy ponytail. She is wearing shorts and a tank top, and her shoulders are streaked with red and blue, the pull and press of fingers and nails. There are scratches on her arms, her legs, circles of red around her ankles.

"What happened to you? What did he do?"

"Nothing," Nika says. Her eyes are as red as Daria's in the sauna, sore and tired from crying. "The car. I think I messed it up driving back. I'm not so good at shifting."

"The car?" Daria says. "Where's Matti? Why didn't he drive?"

"I left the tent there. It belongs to his father. I just sat there all day yesterday and then I got in the car and left everything. He'll be mad."

"No one's mad. You're safe," Daria says, touching her daughter's shoulders, just resting her open palms on top of them so as not to squeeze the bruises. "And Matti? Is he safe? Or—not safe?"

"Not safe."

"Does he need help?"

Nika shakes her head.

"Is he dead?" Daria asks her daughter, because she can think of no other way to say it, and Nika nods. Daria walks them to the kitchen before she asks her daughter how. She puts on the kettle, looks at the clock. Paavo won't be home for hours. The police won't bother with her while she's alone, unable to talk to them. Which is good because the story, when Nika tells it, takes a long time. Her breath won't come. Her throat tightens, mucus runs over her top lip and she lets it, swipes it with her tongue, until her mother takes a box of tissues from the bathroom and cleans her daughter's face. The story spills out slowly, and Daria can't help calculating the length and breadth of it, the number of words, the way it contains as much as her daughter has told her in years. It is a story that starts with two teenagers in the forest, a midsummer bonfire, a package of sausages to roast on sticks and a case of beer. It was after midnight before the sun threatened to set, sunk rind-deep in the lake they had camped beside. They knew it would slip under and be up again in less than an hour, but there was still a sadness to the moment, that the sun would drown itself for even an instant. They were both full of sausage and beer when Matti suggested they swim toward it, the orange rim above the water. They stripped off their clothes and ran in. The water was frigid. They swam toward the sun, into the middle of the lake, and when Matti started to cramp, Nika was the only thing he had to hang on to. He panicked, thrashed in the water, tried to lever himself onto her shoulders and ended up pulling them both under. He grabbed at her legs, her ankles, and she kicked out instinctively, swallowing lake water and trying to scream to him to stop. He was too scared to listen, unable to make his body obey him. He had had them both under for over a minute, sinking, pulling Nika down with him, when Nika started kicking. She found his shoulder first, then his face, over and over until he let go and she shot up to the surface. Three breaths and she went down again, Nika told her mother, looking for him, to grab him and pull him up. He was twice her size, but if he didn't struggle she could have gotten him back to shore. She dove and dove and couldn't find him. The sun went down and the deeper Nika dove the more nothing she found. Her lungs were aching, her feet were numb and sore where she'd kicked him, and when a pressure began to poke at her side, she could think of nothing to do but swim to shore. She swam out two more times that night, until she didn't trust herself to make it there and back again, and found nothing. The next day she spent sitting on a fallen log by their burnt-out fire. She started drinking a beer, dumped it on the ashes. Opened another one, took a swallow. Matti's cell phone, still in the pocket of the jeans he'd left crumpled in the mud at the edge of the lake, rang eight times in an hour. On the ninth Nika pulled it out and threw it in the lake. The next night was cold enough Nika wrapped herself in Paavo's old sleeping bag and must have slept, because she woke up propped against the log, and decided she had to leave. "I killed him," Nika tells her mother. The kettle has burbled and then quieted, the hush before the boil. Daria has picked it up before it could scream, but hasn't poured the water. She only stands there, her arm shaking with the weight of the kettle, the burner still glowing.

"You didn't kill him."

"I kicked him and he drowned."

"You didn't have a choice."

"His parents will hate me."

"No one will hate you. It's not a crime. Not being able to save someone."

"They'll hate me," Nika says, and Daria turns back to the stove, sets the kettle down, turns the heat off. She is not sure why this is the thing that troubles Nika so desperately until Nika describes a whole life Daria has known nothing about, helping pick currants off the bushes in Matti's family's backyard and bottling their juice. She has helped Matti's sister braid hair and try on makeup. Matti's father has invited her mushroom-picking in the autumn. She has helped Matti's mother tidy the kitchen after meals. His family has a piano, and Nika has played a little, only what she remembers from school, since she has never had an instrument to play at home. "His parents," Nika says. "They've been so good to me. They'll hate me now."

"They won't," Daria says, taking mugs from the cupboard, teabags from the tin.

"How could they not?"

"If you don't tell them," Daria says. "If you never tell anyone." She steeps the tea, brings the cups to the table with a little ceramic dish in the shape of a teapot, printed with roses and stained brown from the seep of old teabags. Nika puts her hands around the mug and shakes her head at sweeteners. Daria sits across from her, lets her tea turn almost black and then lifts out the bag. Nika doesn't move, and Daria lifts hers out as well, lets them slump soggily in the little dish.

"You will say you were eating, drinking, watching the sun go down," Daria says, as soothingly but matter-of-fact as she can. "Matti went swimming. Only him. He went far out and then you couldn't see him anymore. You shouted and you swam and you dove until you couldn't breathe. It's true. All this is true."

Nika gestures at her scratched shoulders, scraped feet.

"You went as far down as you could, seaweed wrapped around your ankles. You almost didn't make it up. You spent the night leaning against a log. How would your shoulders not be scraped? Besides, you'll change clothes. A long-sleeved shirt, jeans. They might never see."

Nika only looks at her, holds her body straighter. She is sore and in pain, and her mother can see her trying to figure out how not to show it, how to walk unhunched toward Matti's parents and be hugged without flinching.

"What will it hurt?" Daria asks. "Nothing. No one."

Nika nods, and Daria does not know what it means, whether Nika agrees, whether she trusts herself to speak.

"It's a good story. It's almost true. And it will hurt everyone so much less. Two families. You can spare two families."

Nika looks for a moment as if she is trying to figure out who the other family is, who besides Matti's parents pick berries in their backyard and laugh together at the same television shows. She realizes that her mother means the two of them and Paavo, or perhaps not Paavo, perhaps only the two of them. Daria tells the story again, spins a tale that is as long as anything she has said to her daughter in a year. She takes more time over it than her announcement to Nika that she'd signed with the agency, staked her hopes on finding an elderly Finnish man who had been too long alone. She fills in the details, the feel of the light, the smell of the water, the horror of seeing Matti disappear beneath the surface of the lake. Nika was the one who was there, the one who knows these things, yet she is leaning forward, hanging on the words of the story she will be expected to tell.

Nika nods. She doesn't speak, but it is a good nod, sharp and decisive. Daria can see the muscles move along her neck. Daria smiles, takes her daughter's hand without speaking. The silence will swallow them, and it will save them whole. She thinks how exciting the story will be for the interpreter, how it will be a momentous task for the man with skin like the peels of new potatoes; how he will pause and lag and struggle to find a way to tell a family that their teenage son is dead and if it is anyone's fault it's his own. The interpreter will struggle for the words, and Daria wonders how many she and Nika already know: *forest, lake, boyfriend, dark, I'm sorry. Metsä, järvi, poikaystävä, pimea, pahoillani.* Daria could ask now, about *olen pahoillani,* whether Nika knows this phrase for a regret so extraordinary that daily language cannot hold it. She could ask, but doesn't. Even if Nika knows the word, it is not now or ever a thing she wants to hear her daughter say.

In the Gulf of Aden, Past the Cape of Guardafui

In Tangier they were childless. At sea north of Algiers, the parents of a tuba prodigy. In Tunis, the parents of a daughter whose wedding featured a flock of ice sculptures: not only swans but cranes, herons, osprey. Geese mate for life, Lucinda and Wil told their fellow passengers on the *Wavecrest*, and the eagles cost as much as their double-occupancy stateroom on the cruise. As the ship sailed between Malta to the north and Tripoli to the south, the sea calm in between, the first formal dinner was scheduled with seatings at seven and eight. Wil and Lucinda unzipped their garment bags to find Wil's dinner jacket had the unmistakable smell of storage, lines pressed stiff along the seams and a mothy cedar smell from the wooden chips tucked in the closets at home. They hooked the hanger on the railing of their private balcony and let the suit flap over the Mediterranean. By dinner, lamb rubbed with mint and rosemary, Wil smelled like salt and wind and a peach sunset over the straits of Gibraltar, and they told their tablemates that their son was a cryptography genius recruited by the NSA at the age of twelve.

"Gunther asked us to send him a postcard from Egypt," Wil said.

"And we said we could do better than that: a postcard for every day of the cruise," Lucinda added. "It's such an interesting part of the world."

Their tablemates, three elderly couples from Britain and Germany, stiff-backed and sparkling in evening wear, nodded. It was indeed an interesting part of the world, they said, and Gunther sounded like an interesting little boy.

"He is," Lucinda nodded fervently. "He is."

Wilbur and Lucinda Voorhuis were both fifty-one, and while Wil's round face carried the number better than his wife's, Lucinda often wore sleeveless dresses that showed off the long, firm muscles of her arms. They were both indeterminate enough to claim a hedgefund manager, a sweet-smelling infant, America's most promising young speed skater. At anchor in Port Said, at the northern edge of the Suez Canal, passengers on the inland river excursion were ferried on buses to Cairo, then on to Giza. The driver played a tape of educational commentary: the carving of the Sphinx in 2650 BC, the long solar boats that carried the Pharaohs into eternity. Wil asked Lucinda for a pen and notepad from her purse and drew a sideways Egyptian with the head of a jackal and a pleated skirt. "Anubis finds Lucinda worthy of paradise," Will wrote in a speech bubble above the jackal's snout. "Her heart is lighter than an osprey's feather." He was showing it to his wife when the elderly woman across the aisle asked if they'd had news yet from their eldest. Lucinda couldn't remember which child the woman was asking about, whether she needed an update on an Olympic bid in handball or the identification of breakages in chromosome 17p13. She wondered, for a wild, fluttering moment, if her real child had in fact typed a note, penned a letter, called the front desk of the Cairo Hilton and asked to be connected to Mr. and Mrs. Voorhuis' room.

"The article's still being vetted," Wil stepped in. "But we're hopeful for the September issue. If not *JAMA*, it looks like *The Lancet* will take it."

"It's quite an accomplishment," the woman said. "I'd never even heard of the condition, and here's a young man who's got it all worked out."

"It's not very common," Wil said.

"Small mercy to those that have it."

"True enough. We're very proud of him."

∞

Wil had once planned to be a doctor, but had transferred to dental school after one semester. "I decided I didn't want that kind of responsibility," he told Lucinda on their first date, drinks in the Plaza in downtown Kansas City. He did a lot of elective oral surgery procedures for which patients paid out of pocket. It was an excellent living, but it would still have been useful for their son to have a doctor for a father. There would have been a camaraderie in the hospitals, the sympathy textured with less condescension, more empathy. Wil had tried, sometimes, when Aaron was in the NICU. "I was in med school for a year," he'd say. "Oral surgeon, now. I can tell you the tongue's as finicky as a spine. Just a tangle of nerves." It made the doctors trade looks over Aaron's head. Lucinda had waited for Wil to catch on, to feel the blush of his own embarrassment, but eight months in, Aaron still in intensive care, Lucinda on an indefinite leave of absence from her job with an insurance firm, she finally asked him to stop. Over cheeseburgers in the hospital cafeteria, she tried to explain the vast distance between a pediatric neurologist and a man who extracted wisdom teeth twelve times per week, however much they might share in the materials of the body, the blood and the white solidity of skull or tooth or jaw.

Wil convinced Lucinda to take a camel ride on the Western Plateau and snapped picture after picture while she swayed uncertainly on the animal's hump. The camel smelled warm and dusty, its hair faintly oily like sheep's wool and full of grit. Lucinda wound her fingers around the tasseled reins and into its brown coat, squeezed her legs tighter. She was wearing white linen against a blue sky, the sand-colored pyramids of Giza ranged behind her. Wil paid the Egyptian photographer for two Polaroids, fitted into paper sleeves that framed the pictures with *Camels!: An Egyptian Tradishon.* "Lovely," the camel-keeper said, as he helped Lucinda back to earth. "How many camels for your woman?" he asked Wil.

"Twenty," Wil said. "You can have her for twenty."

The camel-keeper frowned. "It was a joke. You are supposed to be offended."

∞

There was a second shore excursion to Alexandria and its new library, glass and steel built with UN money. The tour lasted two hours, which gave Wil time to come up with sixteen ways to burn the building down. "I shall incinerate the common heritage of man," he whispered, as the tour guide ushered them past a bank of computers.

"Stop," Lucinda said. Between the information about modern methods of moisture control, about the Greco-Roman heritage of El Iskandariya and the causeway that linked the Cape of Figs to the old Pharos Lighthouse, about their expanding multitude of brilliant children, it felt like more knowledge than she could handle. She kicked Wil in the shin when he spoke about their son, a boy with straw-colored hair like his mother's and wide, shining eyes like no one they'd known. Lucinda apologized after dinner, because Wil had for once said no more than what was true.

It was the first real vacation they'd taken since the birth, and of course everyone had asked what they were doing with Aaron, what arrangements they'd made, as if he were mail to be picked up or a plant to be watered. There's a good facility in Olathe, they said, wondering how to explain without feeling like they'd taken their son to be kenneled like a dog. They'd been looking at the facility anyway, worrying about a time they might no longer be able to care for him. Children with more awareness, they'd been told, should be eased into institutionalization. With Aaron, nobody knew. He followed things with his eyes, sometimes. He smiled at people who entered his field of vision. He had learned to swallow, eventually, and to roll over unassisted. He was ten years old, and no one had any idea how long he might live.

Sometimes Lucinda could spend an hour touching the soft bottoms of his feet, the distinct whorls of toe prints that walking had never rubbed away. His feet were beautiful and very wrong, marked with raised patterns never meant to last. Once a year she would ink his feet, press them to a piece of white posterboard. She hung the prints in a long line down the basement stairwell.

The afternoon the ship entered the Suez, the Voorhuises kept to themselves, took photographs of each other, singly, posed with the brown geometry of the canal, the tall, vertical walls. One of the leisure coordinators saw them and offered to take a picture of them both together. They put their arms around each other's waist and smiled. At the moment the leisure coordinator snapped the picture, a maintenance crew appeared on the crest of the shore, on the Sinai side, above Lucinda's left shoulder. The coordinator handed the digital camera back to them and watched them call up the shot. "Is it okay?" she asked. "Do you want me to try again? Are you enjoying yourselves?"

"Yes. No. Immensely," Wil answered, and the leisure coordinator left them alone.

Out the other side of the Suez, skirting the Saudi peninsula, Lucinda imagined she could feel the spray of the Red Sea coating her skin with a layer of brine so salty a lick across her hand would make her lips purse with the bitterness. She could feel it crust along her hair, brackish and saline, and she showered morning, night, and midday. She and Wil spent two hours on a sunny afternoon inside the ship's boutique arguing over souvenirs and postcards: who to send to, which pictures, how many, how much. They bought nearly fifty cards, and they knew they looked green, like people who never traveled sending mail to everyone they'd ever met because there might not be an opportunity like this again. This was essentially true, and Lucinda only had the energy for so much deception. That evening they ate room service, the sliding doors open and the table wedged halfway through. Wil ate on the balcony and Lucinda inside and the wind yelped through the open space. The evening after that, 120 kilometers off the northeastern tip of Somalia, in the Gulf of Aden, the ship was hijacked.

"Pirates," the chambermaid told them. "We're asking everyone to stay in their staterooms until the matter is resolved."

Wil laughed and the chambermaid stared. "Wait," Wil said. "Really?"

"The nonessential staff has been assembled in the main dining room, and we're asking everyone else to stay in their quarters."

"We'll just sit tight then," Lucinda said.

"Yes, please. Sit tight. The passengers may be . . . mustered, later, in the dining room, according to demands. We will come and tell you if you need to leave. It might be good to be ready." Kristina, the maid assigned to Ocean View Suite D147, was tall and blond, her English polished. Wil thought it was a mark of the quality of the cruise line that they employed such handsome, educated women, who wore lapel pins of the flags of countries whose languages they spoke. Kristina's pins ran along the base of her white collar, just above her tailored black dress. Sweden, Norway, Denmark, Germany, France, the United Kingdom. Still, she used words like "muster" uncertainly, as if she'd recently been briefed, as if she heard herself now saying things she had never thought she'd need to know.

"We'll bring you more details as we have them," Kristina said. "Do you need anything?"

"No, we're fine," Lucinda said, and when Kristina was gone Wil started to laugh again.

"It isn't funny."

"Of course it is. Pirates. This'll be something for the Christmas letter. 'Lucy mouthed off to one of their parrots and got beaten with a peg leg.'"

"Wil."

"Pirates, Lucy. What else are we supposed to do?"

They had woken an hour earlier to a sound low and piercing, a painful boom that rattled the room. It sounded twice more and when the sound died away Lucinda and Wil were both sitting rigidly upright, startled out of sleep so quickly they each thought they could hear the other's heart hammer. The ship was grinding beneath them, a thrum that increased in frequency until there was a strange vibration in the feel of the air, the floor beneath them, the walls and windows. The ship steered sharply portside, but was so large Lucinda and Wil could only mark the direction by poking their heads out the sliding doors and examining the shifting wake behind them. There was obviously something to be gotten away from, but it seemed impossible that the *Wavecrest* could be maneuverable enough, quick enough to do it. Between and after the booming noise was a lighter crackle, more familiar, the weaponry of video games or films. They tried to wonder in the quieter spaces if someone was simply watching a movie too loudly next door.

"An acoustic—bang. Bam. It is used as a deterrent," Kristina had been able to tell them when they opened the door to her. They were wrapped in plush *Wavecrest* bathrobes over their pajamas, Lucinda rolling her bare feet backward and forward on her toes. "The ships in this area all carry them."

"But what does it do? The booming noise?"

"It is loud. That's what it does."

"It's not a real weapon."

"Not a weapon, no. A deterrent only."

"And it hasn't deterred them."

"Please remain calm."

"They have weapons? Real ones?"

"It is a temporary situation, madam. They are only pirates. Somalis. They have been hijacking UN relief ships for rice. There has been a lot of food coming through this region, after the tsunami."

"But we're not carrying rice."

"No. This is a new thing for the pirates. We assume they want money. Please don't worry."

Wil and Lucinda dressed with a faint sense of excitement. They pondered the appropriate footwear for a hostage situation. They turned on the bedside lamp, brushed their teeth in the bathroom, and were modestly surprised to find that their room functioned the way it always had. Wil sorted through the minibar, the gift basket that had been placed on their bed at the start of the cruise, and they shared an orange and a packet of cheese crackers. They were still hungry, but thought they should ration. They watched the water outside, the whisk of large speedboats skirting the side of the *Wavecrest* beneath them, the faint smell of smoke. They could see small people, clearly armed, porcupined with the slight black quills of weapons six decks below their balcony. But the pirates didn't do anything, just patrolled around and around, and sooner than Wil and Lucinda expected, the novelty had worn off. "Would it be wrong to watch television?" Wil asked.

At noon they split a packet of cashews and turned on the wall-mounted television set. There was nothing but static, the first sign within the room that anything was amiss. Lucinda checked the telephone and heard no dial tone. Every so often there was the sound of footsteps moving quickly down the hall outside. The soft carpet made it impossible to tell whether they were Kristina's sensible heels, the sandals of a wayward passenger, the heavy boots of a Somali pirate. Lucinda gathered all the cups and glasses in the room, the ice bucket, the flower vase, to fill them all with water from the bathroom sink. It was what you did during tornado season, or before a bad blizzard that might freeze the pipes. It might as well be done during a pirate attack. She lined up the plastic bathroom cups and wine glasses along the vanity counter in the main room, left the vase by the toilet so it could be used for flushing. Lucinda wondered if it would be rather cavalier to take a shower. They might still be mustered. They might still be killed.

Midafternoon they both took out books and started to read, Lucinda a mystery and Wil a historical novel about naval warfare. Lucinda opened the balcony door. "It's too stuffy in here," she said. "And the glass would hardly stop bullets anyway." At dinner time they ate raisins and Oreos and went to bed immediately after sunset. "I'm going to shower tomorrow," Lucinda said. "I don't care. I need something to do." They lay in bed and listened to the silence. The buzz of the speedboats had stopped, and Wil wondered how much fuel the small boats carried, how far offshore they all were and where they were headed. Lucinda thought she could hear the rustling of other passengers, imagined tapping out urgent messages room to room in Morse code. She wished she knew Morse code. She imagined the pirates dismantling the diving board at the swimming pool on deck eight, tying it down over the starboard railing like a seesaw and forcing all 316 passengers off it one by one. She waited for the splash of falling bodies.

A few days after Aaron's first birthday, Wil had quietly suggested they might try for another child. He refrained from saying a better one. Aaron's birth had taken three rounds of IVF, years of trying for a baby in every old-fashioned way they knew how. Adoption, Wil suggested, but Lucinda shook her head. "I'm tired," she said. "I don't think you understand how tired I am." Any object as incapable as Aaron—stones, sticks, cinder blocks—needed nothing. Aaron had a body's necessities, a blind kitten's, a featherless bird's, the naked pink jelly-bean of a marsupial baby. His needs were complex and his inability to meet them total.

Once, at work, Wil overheard his nurse anesthetist wondering aloud why Aaron hadn't been aborted. "We didn't know," he explained to her. "There was no way to know until after he was born." Later he wondered if he should have fired her, told her they would have kept Aaron either way, that he was their child and that was enough. He wondered if that was what Lucinda would have said, if she would have meant it. If he had known, he would not have wanted his son, this particular son. He knew this about himself, and thought that if he could ask Lucinda how she felt he would know a great deal more about her, about her long, mysterious days at home.

The next day Lucinda and Wil both showered, put their hostage outfits back on. They each drank a cup of tap water. They'd decided to husband their resources, the Perrier, the Evian in the mini-fridge. Everything in the room still worked except the television. Lucinda even blow-dried her hair. "We could write our postcards," she suggested. "No sense putting it off."

"Because we've got nothing else to do, or because we're going to die?"

Lucinda threw a pillow at his head.

"Are we really doing twenty-one for Aaron?" he asked.

"I said I would. One for every day of the trip."

"You know he won't—"

"I know. I said I would."

Aaron had been born with his brain unfurrowed, lissencephalic, as slick and smooth as the greasy inside of a shell. The MRI confirmed the lack of creases and ruts, troughs or ridges. Knowledge must live in the washes of the brain, Wil decided when the doctors told them that Aaron might or might not learn to swallow. They received printouts of the MRI, filed them away in an accordion folder penciled "Aaron, Medical," in the basement. By six months the paperwork had exploded into a second folder and Wil, refiling, had taken one of the black-and-white pictures. He kept it folded in his wallet. Every day since Tangier he had imagined taking it out at dinner, over the appetizers, shrimp cocktail, mussels in a white wine curry. They cracked shells, pried the gray flesh out with narrow forks, and Wil imagined opening his wallet. This, he imagined saying, is my son. His name is Aaron. He has eyes the color of wonder and a brain as slack and damp as an oyster.

They divided the postcards into stacks, enough for Wil to write to his staff, the dental hygienists and the front office, to his relatives and to a handful of mutual friends. Lucinda took enough for her family, a few neighbors, twenty-one for their son.

"Which do you think for my sister?" Lucinda asked. "A pyramid or a Sphinx?"

"Pyramid," Wil answered, and wrote to his own sister. He picked a photo of the Biblioteca Alexandria and wrote: *Dear Joan, The trip has been amazing. We're currently being held hostage by pirates, but if you receive this it means the situation's sorted itself out just fine. Hope you weren't worried.* He was almost out of room. *The food's been great. Love, Wil,* he wrote, and looked up her address in the notebook Lucinda had brought.

Lucinda wrote doggedly, flipping over new cards long after Wil had finished with his. She kept putting the pen down, shaking her hand out, cracking her knuckles. It looked both theatrical and weary. The sun was dropping and Wil flipped on the overhead switch for his wife. Nothing happened. He tried the bedside lamps, the bulbs over the vanity mirror, the bathroom light. "I'll finish these on the balcony, then," Lucinda said, gripping her pen more tightly. "While there's still a little sun."

She sat on one of their two lounge chairs and Wil thought about joining her, wondered if he was welcome. The sea was quiet, the showy sparkle of the sunset giving way to darker blue and black, faint slashes of light on the swells rather than a field of sequins. There were walls on either side of the balcony, two thirds of the height to the deck above. Wil thought that could be a project for tomorrow, climbing over or around the partitions, sharing crackers with their neighbors and planning a resistance.

The room was hot and Wil kicked the comforter to the floor. He heard Lucinda trip on it as she came to bed, late, the night nearly moonless outside. He heard her start to pull the drapes, and asked her to leave the doors cracked open. "We need some air in here," he said.

Lucinda slept late the next morning, the third of the lockdown, and Wil was restless. He ate a whole packet of gummy fruit snacks by himself, then felt guilty. He re-read the ship welcome magazine and the list of ship's programming for February 11th, the day before the hijacking. There had been a lecture on the desert of Wadi Rum he had meant to attend and forgotten. The room was bright, but Lucinda simply rolled over, pushed her head farther into the pillow. Her postcards were stacked on the vanity, rubber-banded neatly. Wil flipped through them: her parents, her sisters, Aaron's homecare aide and physical therapist. Twenty-one for Aaron.

Dear Aaron,

Tangier was exciting, lots of palm and fruit trees, but a little hard to take. Crowds of people selling stuff on the docks, not wanting to take no for an answer. I got whistled at twice, though, which isn't bad for your decrepit old mother. Guess I don't mind. Wish you were here. Love, Mom.

There were other, simpler ones. *Passed through the canal today,* she'd written on a picture of Al Isma'iliyah, at the southern end of the Suez. *Hope you're well. Love, Mom.*

Dear Aaron,

This is the city of Al Aq'abah. It's in Jordan, it's a port, and you'll never know what either of those mean. Love, Mom.

Dear Aaron,

Your father's on the couch reading his naval war books. He's wearing socks and sandals and every so often he tilts his rear to the side and farts quietly like he thinks I won't notice. I'm sure he misses you. Love, Mom.

Dear Aaron,

Blah. Blah blah blah de blahdedy blah blah blah. Blaaaaaaaaaaaaaaaaaaaaaah. Blahblahblahblah. Love, Mom.

Dear Aaron,

Your brain is atrophic. You have a total lack of sulci and gyri in the coronal and transverse sections of your brain. The corpus callosum is absent. Your condition is the result of a de novo chromosomal aberration. You want to hear some more words you don't know? How about these: fish, dog, sky, ice cream, sun, moon, mom, dad, child. Your dad and I were karyotyped and we were fine—no monosomy of the terminal segment of the short arm of the seventeenth chromosome, especially band 17p13. So no one knows what the hell happened to you. Love, Mom.

 Dear Aaron,

 Sometimes I think about giving you too much of the Depakote. I wonder how many you'd swallow. You've gotten good at it, swallowing. I think about these things and I'm four thousand miles away and I'm still thinking about them. I love you desperately.

Wil put them all back in order, the corners squared and the rubber band tight. He waited for his wife to wake and when she did he gave her two snack-size bags of potato chips and told her they had more. They didn't, but he'd appointed himself head of rations, and she didn't have to know. He dug through their bags and found a squashed granola bar, a bag of something called Meganuts from a market stall in Cairo, a spare box of TicTacs in Lucinda's toiletry bag, a long rope of beef jerky in his carry-on from the plane. He piled the new food into the gift basket and held the jerky up like a trophy. "A whole new food group," he announced.

"I'm staying in bed today. I'm conserving energy. A body at rest requires minimal calories."

"Suit yourself. I'm thinking about swinging out over the edge of the balcony and planning a resistance movement with the neighbors."

"Good luck. The Robertsons are what? Eighty-something at least and the Schullers are three thousand and six."

Lucinda, as she said she would, napped most of the afternoon, and after sunset could manage only a confused doze, slipping in and out of dreams. She woke up at one in the morning certain that she was going to die. She would perish 120 kilometers off the Cape of Guardafui in the Arabian Sea, and her body would never make it home. She swung her feet off the side of the bed and felt in the instant they touched the floor that it had to be true.

"We're going to die," she whispered to her husband.

Wil exhaled, a burbling sigh that squeezed through the congestion in his nose. He turned away and did not wake up. His head tipped backward of its own accord, lengthening and baring his throat. The Adam's apple was tight and round, pushing against the skin. He hadn't shaved since the hijacking, and his throat bristled blond and white along and below his jawline, patches of rough scattering almost down to his collar. She had only ever known him meticulously clean-shaven. Lucinda looked down at her husband, asleep in the bed that was bolted solidly to the wall and floor. She wanted to ask him who he was. I've realized you're a mystery, she wanted to say. I've lived ten years surrounded by strangers. My funny husband and my unknowable son.

Then she thought, the postcards. The postcards for Aaron. They were still sitting in a stack, neatly addressed to their house in Overland Park. If she and Wil had made it home, she thought, they probably would have beaten the postcards. They would have picked Aaron up from the Sunflower Home in Olathe and strapped him into the van and said, don't worry, your presents are on the way. Postcards and magnets and a rubber model of the Sphinx and a plush camel and a plastic cruise ship. Baby toys, she would apologize. I know you're ten but I don't know what else to get for you. I don't know what you want.

She picked up the cards on the vanity, separated out the ones to her son, and walked to the balcony. She ripped the postcards in half, one by one, and scattered them; they fluttered and fell, caught by the railings and walls of balconies below, by updrafts and breezes. They flew and sank and one by one they disappeared. She was going to die, after all, and did not want anyone to see these postcards, to read them or touch them or feel they knew then something about her, about the boy she meant to send them to.

If there was to be at some point a separation of sheep and lambs, wheat and chaff, the passengers who would be spared and those who would be executed, she thought she and Wil should volunteer themselves. They were qualified hostages, years of experience. They wouldn't protest. They could be shuttled and shuffled and they would do it with, if not love, a numb contentment. In the language of her homecare support group, the cruise had had a special name, "respite care," not for Aaron but for her, a term created to make the caregivers feel less guilty, to remind them that their own sanity was of importance. Sitting in another room and reading a magazine while someone else listened to your child scream was respite care. Going to a matinee while someone else suctioned out his aspirated saliva was respite care. Her support group had been jealous only of the money that allowed such an extravagant trip; they did not question the necessity of departure. Respite care, they knew, made you infinitely less likely to smother your own child, to hit them, hurt them, hasten them out of this world. Only Lucinda had looked askance at the idea, its implication of necessity, its acknowledgment of her darker desires.

Late the next afternoon, the fourth, the phone rang. Wil answered it, tried to steel himself for a piratical summons, for a foreign accent that would command his presence at a great slaughter of the rich and elderly. But it was only Kristina. "Arrangements have been made," she said. "An agreement struck." She came down hard, ringingly, on the "struck," proud to know the word, to deliver such fine news to her huddled charges. "We are headed for the Seychelles, not Mombasa. A little farther east, perhaps thirteen hours. You will be able to disembark by tomorrow morning."

"What happened? What's the agreement?"

"I am afraid I can't give any details, Mr. Voorhuis, and I have many more calls to make."

"So it's over, just like that?"

"More or less. We hope you understand that Gilded Hemisphere Lines is very grateful for your patience with the situation."

Wil found Lucinda hunched over on the end of a balcony lounge chair where she'd spent most of the day, her hands wrapped under her elbows. He fit himself in behind her, his legs on either side, his chest pressed against her spine. "We're headed for the Seychelles," he said. "We'll be off the boat by tomorrow morning."

"Who called?"

"Kristina. We're all going to be fine, Lucy." She said nothing, and he wrapped his arms around her chest. She didn't turn to look at him.

"We'll be home day after tomorrow," Wil said. "I'll bet you anything. The cruiseline will be desperate to get us all back to our own countries before we can talk to the press. We'll be in the Seychelles tomorrow morning, then a flight to London. A transfer to Newark, or a direct to St. Louis. A hop, skip and a jump to Kansas City." Her silence pushed him on. "We'll pick up the car at long-term parking, go get the kids. All eight of them. God, it's amazing, the triplets—I have to say, I was none too excited about miming when they started it up, those glass boxes and invisible ropes, but by all accounts they've got real talent. Even in those little berets, striped shirts like a chain gang. And our youngest—"

"Stop, Wil. Please, stop."

"You don't want to, anymore?"

"It's not fun anymore. It's not funny."

"Okay, whatever you want. No more kids."

That still seemed the wrong thing to say, and Wil eased out of the chair to bring them a feast of leftover food, gummy worms, pretzels, two green apples and a bag of chalky dinner mints. Night came on, but the electricity hummed back to life, and in ones and twos and twelves the dark water was lit with rectangles of yellow light, a grid of windows and doors in the sea, the outlines of 316 people living safely in the side of a leviathan. "We'll all be home in a couple of days," Wil said. "All of us."

"All of us," Lucinda said. "Home."

"Home."

"Yes. We'll be home."

ACKNOWLEDGMENTS

These stories, sometimes in slightly different form, first appeared in the following publications:

The Southern Review: "Zolaria"
Blackbird: "It Looks Like This"
Passages North: "Zero Conditional"
Tin House: "Going to Estonia"
Epoch: "World Champion Cow of the Insane"
Prairie Schooner and *The Pushcart Prize XXXV: Best of the Small Presses:* "Steal Small"
The Cincinnati Review: "Embodied"
The Paris Review: "At the Zoo"
West Branch: "The Lion Gate"
Third Coast and *The PEN/O. Henry Prize Stories 2009:* "This Is Not Your City"
The Gettysburg Review: "In the Gulf of Aden, Past the Cape of Guardafui"

More people than I could possibly list have contributed to this book, in ways large and small. I've stolen punch lines, couches, fish tanks, translations, and more. Thanks to all those who have fed me with your friendship, your conversation, your wisdom, your humor. I hope you know who you are.

I'm especially thankful to everyone who read these stories and not only helped make them better, but made me a better writer:

To my teachers, including Ron Carlson, Melissa Pritchard, T.M. McNally, Erin McGraw, Kim McMullen, and Judith DeWoskin.

To the whole Arizona State University MFA crowd, but especially Beth Staples, Katie Cortese, Liz Weld, Marian Crotty, Elizabyth Hiscox, Douglas Jones, Matthew Frank.

To other writerly friends: Ander Monson, Austin Bunn, Sarah Stella.

To all the editors who published (and improved) my work in their literary magazines and anthologies, particularly Brock Clarke.

Effusive thanks to Sarah Gorham and everybody at Sarabande, who not only do amazing work, but came riding up as knights in shining armor for this particular book. Thank you to Judy Heiblum, trusted advisor and advocate, and to Pamela Holway, for patience and good counsel.

For their financial support, a deep thank you to Grand Valley State University, Arizona State University, The Virginia G. Piper Center for Creative Writing at Arizona State University, Theresa A. Wilhoit, the Bread Loaf Writers' Conference, the Sewanee Writers' Conference, and *The Paris Review*.

Lastly, I'm grateful to my parents and my sister Mary, who have been there from the beginning with love, support, and good books to read. And to Todd Kaneko: great writer, great editor, and Master of the Atomic Heart Punch.

W. Todd Kaneko

CAITLIN HORROCKS lives in Michigan, by way of Ohio, Arizona, England, Finland, and the Czech Republic. Her stories have appeared in *The PEN/O. Henry Prize Stories 2009, The Best American Short Stories 2011, The Pushcart Prize XXXV, The Paris Review, Tin House,* and *The Southern Review.* Recently, she won the $10,000 Plimpton Prize from *The Paris Review.* She teaches at Grand Valley State University.